HERE WE GO!

Kelvin MacGregor

HERE WE GO!

RED
FOX

A Red Fox Book

Published by Random House Children's Books
20 Vauxhall Bridge Road, London SW1V 2SA

A division of The Random House Group Ltd
London Melbourne Sydney Auckland
Johannesburg and agencies throughout the world

1 3 5 7 9 10 8 6 4 2

First published in Great Britain by
Red Fox 2000

Printed and bound in Denmark by
Nørhaven A/S, Viborg

Papers used by Random House Group Ltd are natural,
recyclable products made from wood grown in sustainable forests.
The manufacturing processes conform to the
environmental regulations of the country of origins.

The Random House Group Limited Reg. No. 954009

www.randomhouse.co.uk

ISBN 0 09 941325 6

For Anita
for everything

My thanks to my agent, Caroline Montgomery – and the rest of the "Crew" – for all they have done for me. And also to Mike Sharland for reading an early draft of the script and wanting to be involved from the beginning.

Thanks to my brilliant editors Anne McNeil and Charlie Sheppard – it's been a pleasure working with you. And to Simon Davis for his excellent cover, Clare Hall-Craggs in publicity, and Elspeth Joy.

Special thanks to my mother, Margaret Mac-Gregor Bower, for making me the way I am. Love you, Maw. And a big thank you to all my family – in France and Britain – for being there for me.

Finally, I want to pay tribute to my wife, Anita. Without your loyal, loving support I would never have written this novel. *Je t'aime, petite Nina.*

Kelvin

1

'. . . And Joey Burns is on the ball! Scotland's man of the match has broken through the French offside trap and he's only got the goalkeeper to beat!

'The referee checks his watch again. He looks over at the linesman. We're in the dying seconds of the World Cup final and the score is still 2-2.

'All eyes are on Joey Burns.

'Barthez races from the six-yard box and makes a desperate dive at Burns' feet. But Scotland's ace attacker quickly sidesteps the Frenchman's last-ditch tackle, and he's now got an open goal!

'Keeping his cool, the grinning centre smacks the ball with all he's got . . . straight in the net!

'Go-o-o-o-o-o-o-o-o-o-o-o-o-o-o-o-o-al!!!

'And the referee has blown the whistle for full-time. It's all over. Scotland have won the World Cup!

'The scenes here today at Hampden Park in Glasgow are unbelievable. The crowd is going crazy. The whole of Scotland will be celebrating this victory tonight. And it's all thanks to hat-trick hero Joey Burns.

'Triumphantly, the Scottish team lift their captain onto their shoulders and carry him over to *collect the trophy.* His *trophy. Television cameras from around the world are zooming in on Burns' handsome smiling face. Everywhere tartan banners sway proudly in the air with personal messages from female fans to Scotland's greatest ever player:*

WE LOVE YOU, JOEY!
BRAVEHEART BURNS!

'Just listen to the crowd cheering . . .'
'Here we go, here we go, here we go-oh . . .'
'We're now going over to our babe-tastic reporter Melanie Anderson who's on the pitch ready to interview the hero himself . . . Joey Burns. *He's all yours, Mel . . . Joey is all yours . . .'*

'Hey, Joey, whadaya wear under yer shorts?'

Having just scored the winner for Scotland in the World Cup final, I'm so caught up with kicking the ball around my back garden that I don't see wee Sally till she's over the fence and startling me stupid with a slide-tackle.

'*Whoa* . . . watch it, Sal!'

Before I know it, we're both slap bang on our backs on the grass, my heart going like crazy as Sally creases up with laughter. She pokes a finger in my ribs in a playful way, really winding me up now.

'So whadaya wear, eh?'

'That does it!' I start tickling her mental 'cause I know how much she hates it, while I tease her about her team, the Ardrossan Girls,

2

getting scudded four-nil in the local derby match on Tuesday night.

'They were – oh! – ah! – s*top it*,' she screams, 'jammy as hell!'

'I heard you've got a really crap goalkeeper.'

'Oh, let go!'

'Here we go, here we go, here we go-*oh* . . .'

Sally Taylor – she's the girl next door – is always jumping over the fence into our garden when she sees me playing with the ball. She doesn't have any brothers or sisters, either, so she's always up for a game. She's mad about football, a real tomboy. Sally's goalkeeper for the Ardrossan Girls team. She let the four goals in.

'We were robbed, OK. Two of the goals should've been disallowed.'

'Yeah, yeah,' I laugh.

She wriggles away from me as I make a grab for her ankle, and gets to her feet giggling, throwing the ball at me so that it stoats me one on the head.

'Ouch! You could get the red card for that.'

'C'mon, Joey, let's practise.'

Sally whips off her blue and white Nike track-suit and dumps it on the grass for goalposts. I notice that underneath it she's got her Scotland strip on again with the big number 1 on her back. She pulls an elastic band out of her pocket and ties back her long black hair. Sometimes – when the sun gets in her eyes and 'cause she's a goalkeeper – Sally wears that old

3

Georgetown baseball cap of mine; the cap she borrowed from me at the start of the season, that she still hasn't given me back yet. The wee cadger.

She's only about fourteen or something, so I don't really mind her coming over and nicking my kit and that. I mean, it's not as if she bugs me or anything, she doesn't. She's dead easy to get on with and chats away like a lad sometimes. And Sally's not a bad goalie – for a girl, I mean – even though her team just got scudded four-nil.

'Didja know,' Sally says as she plays keepy-up with the ball while we warm up, 'that a lot of top football totty wear lucky pants on match days?' She knocks the ball over to me. 'Ya wearin' anything special for the cup final?'

'Naw, just the usual,' I say – not wanting to say anything. 'Just the same pants that I always wear.'

'What, no lucky Calvin's for *hot dates*?'

'They're all the same, my pants. My maw buys them for me . . . I mean, I tell her what colour I want and that . . .' Jeez, I can't believe we're talking about this. I mean, what does it matter what kind of kecks you wear? Nobody's even looking when you're getting into your strip. Not really. *No way*, mate. We're too busy talking about the game and that.

A few minutes later, Sally says, 'Ya think we'll win the cup?'

'Well, that's the game plan,' I tell her.

'Aye, we'd better 'cause the whole school's going, y'know. Millglen Ah-kah-day-may, *yo*!'

'The whole school, eh? All the girls? I can't lose then . . .'

'Dream on, pal. Just try and score some goals.'

I shake my head then hit the ball. 'And there's me thinking, Sal, that I'm the star striker who broke the school's record this season. That's twenty-five goals, in case yer counting.'

'As if you'd let me forget . . .' Sally sighs, shifting her tracksuit goalposts closer together. 'And it's twenty-three goals, by the way.'

Sal and me go to Millglen Academy in Ard-rossan, though I'm two years above her, like. My team is in the Ayrshire Schools Cup final and we're playing against Woodside Academy from Largs a week next Wednesday night. The game is being held in our town at the Ardrossan Rovers' ground. We're just down the road from Largs on the West Coast of Scotland – sort of level on the map with Glasgow, but way over on the left facing the Isle of Arran – so it's a bit of a local game for us.

Ardrossan's quite a small town really, when you think about it. I mean, it's got a harbour and beaches and shops and everything – but it's kind of small when you compare it with a big city like Glasgow. To be honest, it's a bit dull and depressing when you live here, but I suppose most towns are when you've lived there all your life.

Don't get me wrong, though. I'm really proud of my home town and I'm chuffed to bits that the cup final is being held here. Rover Park is a real football ground, you know, with changing rooms and a stand and a hot pie shop and advertisement barriers and turnstiles to get in. Usually we just kick the ball around open playing fields with the old kitbags piled up at the touchline.

'Ya gettin' all excited?' Sally asks, excitement showing on her face.

'Of course. Wouldn't you be . . . if the scout for Ardrossan Rovers was coming to watch you play?' I add slowly, unable to hold the news in any longer.

'Wow! Way to go, Joey!' Sally starts climbing all over me as if I've just scored a goal on the telly. 'Why didn'tcha tell me before?'

''Cause I've only just found out myself . . . C'mon, Sally,' I say, trying to get away. 'Get back in goals.'

'It's a shame your dad won't be there to see you,' she beams. 'He would've been dead proud of . . . Oh, Joey. I'm sorry.' She lets go of me. 'I never meant it that way.'

'It's OK,' I say.

There's a pause and Sally lowers her eyes and then looks straight at me. She seems to sense my unease 'cause she gently takes my hand and says, 'Are you sure?' She's getting really upset about it. She's not just being nice to me, I can tell. I look at Sally, feeling, I don't know what inside, but *nice*. She's really nice sometimes, really cares about other people.

I say, 'Forget about it, Sal. I know it's only been a few weeks.'

My dad's dead now. He was an alcoholic. A bad one. It was the drink that killed him in the end, after years and years of making my mum's life a misery. He drowned in the harbour. He fell in by accident one night when he was drunk. He was always drunk. It was in all the local papers and everything. My dad used to be a docker. That's the tragic irony of it all. Redundancy wasn't enough, the harbour had to go and kill him as well. He was out of work for years, my dad, that's why he became an alky. He was only forty something. These last few weeks have been terrible for my mum and me. We're still trying to get over it; still trying to get used to him not being here any more. We still miss him.

It's hard to believe that he was once the most promising football talent in this part of Ayrshire – but I've seen all the old photos, the proof that he looked well-fit in his black-and-white striped Ardrossan Rovers strip before the beer gut cut short his big chance of a professional career with Glasgow Rangers.

What happened, Dad? Where did it all go wrong?

It was my dad who lined up the scout for

Ardrossan Rovers, but he never told me. I only found out today when my mum saw the Rovers' trainer in town. They're thinking about taking me on when I leave school in the summer. Two months – only two months till the end of June and I'm a free man at last! That's if I get a job, of course, 'cause the Rovers are only a junior league team made up of joiners and plumbers and dockers and that. You don't get paid like professional players, see, and my mum says if I don't get a good job I've got to stay on for sixth year and get better qualifications. I only got four Standard Grades last year because I was apparently training too much and not studying enough. That's what my maw and my teachers say, anyway. But there's a good chance I might get in the Ardrossan Rovers team now 'cause Wullie Watson, their trainer, thinks I'm good. First team good. That's what he told my mum. And let's face it: he knows more about football than teachers and maws and *girls*.

'The Rovers are thinking of signing me up for next season,' I tell Sally, smiling sadly. 'So hands off the hot property.'

'Yer sizzling, Joey Burns. *Sizzling*. I've always known you were the most talented football totty in Ayrshire! What else did the trainer say, hotshot?'

I love it when she gets all excited about something. I don't know why I do, but I do. She gets so passionate when we talk about football sometimes.

'It's the first step to turning pro, y'know. I could have my pick of teams when I'm with the Rovers.'

'Ya better not forget me, Burnsie, when yer rich and famous and playing for Ayr United.'

'No chance, pal. Ayr couldn't afford me. I'll be playing for Killie.'

'You wish.' She grabs me by the scruff. 'And stop dissin' ma team.'

My dream, see, is to turn professional with Kilmarnock FC. They're the best football team in Scotland as far as I'm concerned. Sally supports poxy Ayr United – can you believe it? They're the other big Ayrshire team, but they're crap compared to Killie. I mean, Killie are always near the top of the Premier League and Ayr are only First Division. Sally and me are deadly rivals on Saturday afternoons before the games get going. You should have seen us at ten to five tonight when the results came up on the telly – when Ayr United got beaten again! I was really ribbing her about it.

I hope Ayr don't get promotion to the Premier League, you know. There would be no living with Sally – living next door – if both teams were playing in the same division.

'So when ya gonna swap scarves and support Killie?' I go on, really rubbing it in.

'I wouldn't support Kilmarnock if ya paid me,' she says, getting all snotty now. 'They're as crap as Man United.'

See what I mean: she goes mental when her

team gets trashed! I'm such a massive Killie supporter you wouldn't believe it. Them and Man United. They're my favourite English team. Of course, Sally supports Liverpool, just to be awkward. We've agreed to disagree about everything.

I ask Sally, all casual like, as I line the ball up for a penalty kick, 'D'you know if Melanie Anderson's going to the game? I heard she's covering it for the school paper.'

'Why the interest?'

'Oh, nothin' . . . Just wonderin'.'

'Ya *don't* fancy Melanie Anderson, do ya?'

'Don't be daft.'

Am I that obvious?

'You fancy her, Joey Burns. I can see it in yer eyes.'

I'm that obvious.

'Are you serious?' I say, really serious.

'Forget it, pal.' Sally whacks the ball at me and, as I duck, it smacks off the garden shed into my dad's old cabbage patch that's starting to grow weeds now. 'You could never score with a babe like Melanie Anderson. She's just not your type.'

'Oh, and what *is* my type,' I call over my shoulder as I go for the ball.

'Well, you're all shy and soppy for a start. That's not gonna impress any footie groupies.'

'She's a—'

'Aye, she's a big snob, too,' Sally goes on

10

before I can get another word in. 'Her and her clique of ugly mug mates.'

'She's all right, Mel is. It's just the crowd she hangs out with who—'

'So it's *Mel* now.' Sally sticks her fingers down her throat. Then she suddenly gets all serious again. 'Ya gonna ask her out?'

'Ask her out? I only asked if she was going to the game.'

'Want some advice?' she calls out, kicking a clothes pole off the pitch.

'Advice – from *you*? You're just a kid!'

'A kid . . .' Sally gives me a dead leg then pretends to headbutt me for a laugh – the good old football hooligan's handshake, eh? 'I'm a girl, too, Joey, in case ya hadn't noticed.'

'Gosh, you're right . . .' I say with fake surprise. 'You're really a girl underneath that Scotland strip.' That's one-nil to me, I'm thinking, as Sally sulks and straightens up her tracksuit goalposts on the grass.

'Grow up, Joey.'

OK, I'll admit that I can be immature for my age sometimes. But I'm only sixteen – well, almost seventeen – well, I will be in a couple of months. I'm not taking a slagging like that without giving anything back in return. No way, *pal*.

'What would you know anyway?' I say carelessly.

Sally's right in there with the boot. 'I know how I'd want a boy to ask me out.'

'I'm not asking anybody out.'

'What if she wants ya to snog her. What'ya gonna do, eh?'

'As if *you* would know anything about snogging. You've never even fancied anyone before.'

'Oh, I know.' She looks at me in a funny way, then she looks away.

See, I knew she's never fancied anyone.

'I know how you feel, Joey.'

Uh oh. She's getting all girlie on me now.

Grinning, I go, 'Just supposing – and I *mean* supposing – that I did fancy someone . . . and I'm only speaking hypothetically here, of course.'

'Of course.'

'So how *would* I go about pulling someone.'

'It's dead easy. First of all ya get matey with her best pal – Lucy Harper, isn't it? So, as soon as yer mates with Lucy Harper, ya start pumpin' her for info about Melanie – ask her if she's got a boyfriend, what she likes, doesn't like *etcetera, etcetera*. And make sure ya drop a few subtle hints – and I mean subtle, Joey Burns – that show yer interested in Melanie yerself. Juicy Lucy'll do the rest.'

Sally studies me for a moment, then shakes her head.

'Just watch out, though . . .'

'Watch out for what?' I say, really interested now.

'My, my . . . aren't you getting hot for

12

someone who doesn't have the hots for someone. Hypothetically speaking, of course.'

'Go on . . . Get on with it!'

'Well,' Sally giggles. 'Just watch out that her best mate doesn't think ya fancy *her*. After all, Juicy Lucy's bound to be wondering why yer hanging around with her, acting all lovey-dovey.'

'Who says I'll be acting all lovey-dovey. With Lucy Harper! Gimme a break!' Lucy Harper's a real heavyweight. Getting matey with Lucy Harper just isn't an option. 'No way,' I say, thinking of Lucy Harper squeezing herself into tight black trousers.

'Trust me, Joey. You'll be acting all lovey-dovey.'

'And that's it?'

'Easy, eh?'

Sally's a regular wee substitute agony aunt, I can see. I mean, how was I supposed to know that you have to get all matey with a girl's best friend first before you ask her out. Life without instructions, eh? Batteries not included. What a bummer!

Diving for the ball, Sally makes a brilliant save. She looks up and beams at me. 'Melanie Anderson, eh? So she's the kind of girl you go for . . .'

'I mean it, Sal. If I get a slagging at school for fancying Melanie Anderson – not that I'm saying I do, mind – I'll know where the story got started. D'ya get me?'

'I get you,' she grins as she glances at her sporty Swatch watch. 'Is that the time already? I'll be late for footie training if I don't hurry.' She grabs her tracksuit off the ground.

'Saturday night? The weekend? I didn't know girls took footie so seriously.'

'I'm dedicated to the cause, pal. Oh,' she says, pulling up her tracker bottoms. 'I forgot to show ya my injury yesterday.'

'What injury?' I ask, wondering what she's on about now.

'My gammy leg, that's what.' Sally drops to her knees, getting all excited as she rolls down her red-and-black Scotland sock and shows me this massive chunk of Elastoplast just above her ankle that's caked with crusty dried blood. 'It's only a scab now,' she says, peeling away the plaster. 'Some big weightlifter from the other team left her stud marks on me. She ripped right into me, the cow. I was lying there like a dead man. Ya should have seen me. There was blood everywhere. I wasn't crying or anything,' she adds quickly, 'but the trainer had to come on and I ended up being substituted. It had to be the big derby match as well when all my mates came down to watch me. I was limping like a real dweeb the next day at school.'

'Nasty,' I say. 'You're lucky you didn't break your leg.'

'My dad says I must have footballer's legs to take a tackle like that.'

Sally's skinny legs are really soft and smooth

looking and look nothing like the footballers' legs I know. Take my best mate Rab Guthrie, for instance, who's the goalkeeper for our team. He's like a werewolf wearing a fur jacket when he takes his top off. He's been shaving since he was twelve – so he told me. The big poser! I suppose with Rab being the school stud and that, it goes with this randy reputation of his for snogging the babes. Me, I only have to shave once a month or something stupid. But that's only because I'm fair-haired and fresh-faced, like.

I look at Sally's leg again. 'That's what ya get for not wearing shin pads,' I tell her.

'I hate shin pads,' she says. 'They make me look like a big Hairy Mary hockey player.' She glances at her watch again. 'Now I've really got to go.' Sally races up the garden path, her big rucksack kitbag bouncing up and down on her back. 'Oh, and Joey,' she shouts, slamming the gate behind her. 'Let me know what happens with yer hot date.'

'Get outta here, ya wee geek!'

Look at her go, legging it down the road without any trace of a dweeby injury. I bet she still thinks she's playing for Scotland in that strip of hers. *Me*, grow up? Sally really cracks me up sometimes.

When I think about it later, Sally's the kind of wee sister I'd like to have; if I was to have one, like. We've known each other for years, practically grown up together. Even our mums are best friends – though that's probably only because we're next-door neighbours. She's a really good laugh, Sally. Always up for loads of laddish stuff and not just football. Go-Karting, pool, bowling, diving off the rocks down Saltcoats harbour; you name it and wee Sally's in there with the boys. I even reckon she'll make some boy a good girlfriend one day. I mean, the biggest problem boys have with some girls is that they don't like football. And you can't say that about wee Sally. She's my biggest fan, you know; that's what her mum told my mum. Sally says she'd even go down to Manchester to watch me if I joined United. I mean, it's dead expensive getting the train down to England and that, especially if you have to stay overnight in a hotel as well. For a girl, Sally sure is mad about football.

Sometimes, though, I wish I had a big sister. So I could really get the inside info on girls and snogging and stuff. You know, what girls are really like when they're not at school. What they get up to in their bedrooms when they're not doing homework or watching telly. If you don't have a big sister, how else are you supposed to know about girls? How are you supposed to find out? I've tried – believe me I have. But I give up. I just don't understand girls. They're strange.

2

At school first thing Monday morning, I decide to let my best mate Rab Guthrie in on the big secret about me and Melanie Anderson. How I fancy her like mental is what I'm going to tell him. How you score with a bird you're too scared to talk to is what I'm going to ask him. I mean, I need some kind of advice here about the sad situation my love life is in at the moment. And let's face it, the old school stud standing over there running a steel comb through the greasiest ginger wig in Scotland – slicked back with just a dab too much Dax hair wax, if you ask me – is an A-student on this very subject.

I've been hanging around in the boys' changing rooms at the gym for about two hours now waiting for Rab Guthrie to finish giving himself a movie star make-over in the mirror. The old Sweaty Betty takes ages to get his look right after P.E., especially when we're off to play mixed doubles next in the break, with the girls' tennis team. Rab Guthrie has usually got two or three babes on the go at the same time – so he tells me – so I suppose he has to work hard at the old well-studied image of his. Come on, Rab, I'm thinking as I repack my bag again and tie my laces for the tenth time. Hurry up, willya! The P.E. class isn't over yet, mate, 'cause I want some real Physical Education from you!

Totally in love with himself now, the big poser pulls on his new black-and-orange baseball jacket with the Giants' logo on the front that he hasn't had off his back since he bought it second-hand up in Glasgow. Only first to third years still wear uniforms at our school, see, 'cause after you get into fourth year they let you wear whatever you want. Unless, of course, you're a posh pupil who takes school seriously or a nerd who doesn't know any better. Me? I'm always decked out in these 'smart' grey trousers 'cause my mum doesn't let me wear jeans to school like Rab, and this 'fashionable' green nylon all-weather jacket with a detachable hood buttoned in at the back of my red neck.

Aye, Rab's into everything all-American these days, you know, and can even speak in a good ol' swank yank drawl, y'all. I mean a French accent is OK if you want to sound *sexzee*, but Rab says you need slangy American if you wanna act cool when you pull. Which is why I'm after a quick tutorial lesson off him now. And why Rab opted out of French for metalwork so he can learn how to customise this red-and-chrome Chevrolet motor he reckons he's going to own by the time he's twenty-one; when he's making his third movie and getting hitched to a supermodel with a foreign accent, I mean.

When Rab finally kisses his plukey pizza-face goodbye in the mirror, I go, 'You've got a desperate man here, Rab. What should I do?'

'Nae problem,' he says in his big deep voice when we get out into the bright sunshine and head toward the tennis courts where the girls play with their tiny skirts halfway up their butts. 'Give her best pal a good snoggin' and she'll soon know what she's missing. Birds always tell their best pals what they're gettin' off guys. Gives them somethin' to gossip aboot when they're putting their slap on in the bog.'

Well, thanks there, Rab. Thanks for that enlightening contribution to the *Joey Burns' Sad Beginner's Guide To Understanding The Opposite Sex – Book One*. Now I know who to go to on my wedding night . . . *Not!* Basically what he's saying is not that far removed from what Sally told me the other day. A mental image of Lucy Harper squeezing herself into those tight black trousers of hers flashes through my mind again. Give her best mate a good snoggin'? *Not-an-option*, Rab. It's just not an option.

Suddenly Rab laughs his poxy puss-face off and goes, 'Lemme know how ya get on, Joey. I want all the details, mate, the whole gory story.'

And there he goes . . . Rab Guthrie, Professor Sexperience himself, away to snog any

19

spare bird who's having a quick fag behind the hedges at the tennis courts.

Later that afternoon, my heart does a bungee jump when I see my big chance to ask Melanie Anderson out as she walks along the corridor toward me without any of her mates in tow.

'Well, hello there, Mel baby . . . It's *me* again! Yes, the sad lad who keeps giving you the psycho stare in class all the time. No, don't mind me drooling over you like a lovesick dork – 'cause that's what I am. Don't waste your time with me, darlin', not when all those other guys are queuing up over there ready to snog you . . .'

Ground swallow me up!

I've just blown my big chance again. Look at her go, strutting her stuff like a catwalk super-model straight into Baldy Wilson's maths class without even a backward glance in my direction. That's what I get for not having the guts to open my big gob. What's a kisser for, eh, if you keep it zipped all the time? Somebody *quick*. Get the vet! Put this poor animal out of his suffering.

Dork.
Dork.
Dork.

We're halfway through another boring B.O. Boyle geography lesson when my eyes wander away from the blackboard again – studying you-know-who over the top of my unputdown-able text book.

Oh, Melanie, why do you make my life so miserable?

The worst is when she catches me glancing in her direction. When she looks back at me, I quickly turn away and pretend to be gazing out the window – my burning mug the colour of beetroot.

She's such a babe, a real boy-magnet. And a natural baby blonde as well. No way is her wig out of one of those Nice 'n' Easy bottles or that Sun-In kit. All the lads fancy Mel, you know. Not just me. But she's a weird kind of girl if you ask me. I mean she's smiley and chatty and natters away to everyone like she's their best mate for life. But not me. No way. Half the time I don't even think Melanie Anderson knows I exist.

I mean, I'm always shouting out the answers to those tough questions Teach spouts out. Same as I'm always showing off with the ball in the playground whenever I see Melanie walking by with her mates. I mean, I try to make a good impression when she's around, try to catch her eye and that, but she doesn't seem to notice me sometimes.

And I'm not a pig-ugly dog, by the way, if that's what you're thinking. No way. I'm actu-ally quite good looking as it goes. No, I'm serious. I'm dead tall, got a good build, blondish hair, beautiful blue eyes . . . well so

Sally told my mum once. She said I look a bit like this Hollywood teen idol who's all the rage just now, if you must know. I swear to God. All the girls at our school are mad about him. Sally's even got posters of him all over her bedroom wall and everything.

It's probably just the blond hair, though, that's brought on all this love god lookey-likey stuff. It's kind of longish at the moment, my wig, and always flopping over my face the way this hotshot actor's does. And, to be honest, I've been kind of, you know, trying to copy him a bit. Ever since Sally said I looked like this Hollywood teen idol I've been trying to act dead cool and heart-throbish at school. The hair. The pose. The patter. *Everything*. There, I admit it. When I've got on my new black Levi 501s and my Calvin Klein T-shirt and I'm down the shops in Saltcoats on a Saturday afternoon, I'm a pure love god. A real practising movie star. I've got it all worked out, you know. How to be a heart-throb in ten easy lessons. See Joey Burns, mate, 'cause he's the man with the plan!

I don't like to brag, really . . . but I'm going to anyway. All the lads think I'm a birrova cool dude now. I'm telling you. And the girls? Well, they just look at me and then they look away and start giggling. I even think Melanie Anderson was eyeing me up once, but I can't be sure 'cause I was too busy checking the inspection date on one of the fire extinguishers when she passed me in the corridor.

To be honest, I've never actually had a girl-friend. I mean, I've snogged chicks before, tongued them down good style behind the tennis courts under the watchful eye of the school stud himself Rab Guthrie. I'm thinking about that time I snogged Jennifer Dunlop, if you must know. I still remember the way she suddenly broke away from me – really gasping for air. She said she had a sore head and then she went rushing away to the nurse for a paracetamol. Maybe it was her first snog and it was too much for her. Aye, that's what I reckon it was. It was my first kiss as well, you know. Not bad, eh? So that means I must be a natural-born *laydeez* man, me.

I think I'd be a good boyfriend actually. Oh, it's terrible. These feelings I've got for Melanie. Call it a crush. Call it the hots. Whatever it is, I just can't stop thinking about Melanie!

3

'Are you lads fit for football training?' Mr Lovett asks us.

Love it Lovett with his English accent that sticks out a mile up here and his thick black wig flicked back in a floppy-fringe job that takes Rab Guthrie two hours to copy with his big sister's crimpers. Old Lovett's the new football coach at our school. He's really just a student teacher on loan from a college in Glasgow on one of those give-the-trainee-teacher-a-shot-in-a-real-school-temporary-work-experience-placement-programme-thingies. He's only about twenty-or-so, we reckon, and because this is his first job he's really enthusiastic about every-thing – especially football training. It was his idea to start up the school paper as well and there's always a weekly match report of all our games to look forward to.

Lovett's even got this dead trendy red adidas tracksuit and new Converse trainers, which shows his dedication to the team, 'cause us lot just wear any old washed-out T-shirts and shorts with the scuffed football boots we've had since the beginning of the season.

I like the coach. So does Rab. So do the rest of the lads. There are fourteen of us in the team, including three substitutes. The result was unanimous: 14-0. So that proves what an all right bloke he is. For a wannabe teacher, I mean. And a Chelsea supporter. Old Love it Lovett doesn't have a specific subject to teach at school and has to fill in for the teachers who are either sick or skiving. So sometimes we get him for modern studies or English or P.E. – but nothing too technical like metalwork or biology or home economics.

He actually took over the football team mid-season when our old coach Auld Uncle Albert retired from the school. Auld Uncle Albert just didn't have the energy or the interest any more like the new team boss has. Love it Lovett's the mastermind behind our blinding cup run that has taken us all the way to the final next week. Pity he wasn't here at the beginning of the season, though, 'cause it's too late to win the league and cup double now.

'No pain, no gain,' Lovett says, grinning, as we space out as far apart on the pitch as we can. 'Squat-jumps and sit-ups first . . .'

Twenty-three.

Twenty-four.

Twenty five.

Phew, the warm-up doesn't half get your heart hammering and the sweat pouring off you! I'm really breathing heavily! But can we not just play football, *sir*?

'Go!' Lovett yells. 'Go, go, go!'

I'm away and zigzagging through the half dozen parking cones the coach has lined up along the pitch. Great practice for dribbling skills when you're jinking round defenders up the wing. But we still haven't got to kick a ball yet, sir!

Lovett yells, 'Go again, Braveheart! Go, go, go!'

The team's nickname for me is 'Braveheart' and I've got Love it Lovett to thank for that – him and old William Wallace. The coach says I play like a real Scot's warrior on the pitch; a right tartan terror, he told me. OK, I'll admit that I can get carried away sometimes when the game gets going. I mean I put everything into the match, so I do. I get really passionate about winning. I give my all for the team. All the lads do. I love football. We all love football. We're a team, aren't we? We want to win. We're gonna win that cup!

The warm-up is over. We're sitting huddled round in a circle on the damp grass as the coach talks us through some tactics for the cup final. It's just a quick breather really before we practice what he's preaching on the pitch.

Mr Lovett smiles at me. 'And we even have a

26

hotshot in the team who's got the whole Ayrshire league talking about him this season . . .'

Jeez, what a cringer! Why does he always go
for me? Everyone must think I'm his favourite
pupil now or something. Lovett seems to have
taken a real shine to me, I don't know why. But
why can't he pick another teacher's pet for a
change!

'Aye, he's a secret Sassenach,' Rab chortles.
'He supports Man United.'

'Better than Chelsea,' I say, knocking the ball
back to the coach. I wish we'd talk about something else now – apart from me!

Lovett pokes me gently in the side with a
parking cone. 'Now you're getting personal,
Joey.'

Not as personal as I'm going to get now . . .

'Ya ever think of turning professional, sir?' I
ask him.

Well, we've all been wondering where he got
the semi-pro practice in. Even though he's only
supposed to be the referee, old Lovett always
manages to wangle his way into the game. He's
got a brilliant shot, you know, and can kick with
both feet, too.

'Only the college team, Joey,' he says,
sounding dead chuffed. He turns, chuckling,
toward the others. 'I wish I was playing in the
cup final with you, lads!'

Rab grins. 'Aye, and I wish I had your MG
sports car, sur. And a licence to have a babe in
the reclining passenger seat with me. I'll

27

transfer with you any time if ya want a shot in goals.'

'Now, Guthrie . . .' Lovett stands up. 'Let's get the game going, lads.'

'Yes, sir!' We all jump to our feet and split up into two sides. And then the teacher/coach/ref/all-round-good-bloke-for-a-Chelsea-and-England-supporter blows the whistle and the game gets going . . .

I'm hovering near the twelve-yard box trying to get away from our muscleman captain Ronnie Cowan, who's been told to mark me out of the game. Old Lovett reckons Woodside Academy will have it in for me 'cause my hotshot reputation has got the whole school league talking about me this season. He said the words, remember, not me. I don't fancy myself *that* much. Well, maybe a little bit. But I can't help it the way everybody's been building me up as the hottest teen player in Ayrshire for years. Anyway, big Ronnie Cowan's doing a pretty good job shadowing me. Until Mikey Parker suddenly passes a beauty to me and I've got the ball at my feet.

And then I'm away! *Boy*, am I away!

I'm storming up the wing, then cutting into the box. One defender, two defenders, three defenders, yeees!!! I'm through with only Rab Guthrie to beat!

'Go-o-o-o-o-o-o-o-o-o-o-o-o-o-oal!!!'

I raise my arm with the age-old signal that

I've scored and a smiling Simon Hill is first in line to congratulate me with a high-five.

'Stoater, Joey.'

The rest of the lads on my side swarm round me as we back-slap each other with the words of encouragement I never get tired of hearing . . .

'What a goal!' Mikey Parker says breathlessly.

'It was a beauty!' Wee Davie Wilson beams.

I say, 'Didja see the way it went scudding in the back of the net! Didja see it, boys?'

'Ya were off the mark there, all right,' Ronnie Cowan grins. 'I'm glad yer in our team, hotshot.'

Rab Guthrie laughs. 'I wish somebody would remind him of that. Yur makin' me look like a free transfer here, Burnsie.'

'Check out my Sidewinder,' I shout as I bend the ball round the defenders' wall with the old Brazilian banana shot trick, way out of Rab's reach into the top right hand corner of the net.

'Go-o-o-o-o-o-o-o-o-o-o-o-o-o-o-al!!!'

I clench my fist as Lovett claps his hands.

'Nice one, Joey.'

Speedy winger Simon Hill weaves his way through the midfield, forcing Ronnie Cowan to run after him and leaving me unmarked. Taking them by surprise, Simon quickly backheels the ball to me and I'm charging for goal!

See, when you're running with the ball at your feet and you're through the defence with just a split-second's decision whether or not to lob the ball over the goalie's head or smack a volley in the top corner of the net or side-foot it into that space there next to the goalpost or just belt it with all you've got and hope for the best . . .

'Go-o-o-o-o-o-o-o-o-o-o-o-o-o-o-o-al!!!'

'Another blinder,' the coach says, smiling. 'You're on top form today, Braveheart. Play like this next week and that cup is ours.'

What a buzz!

What a buzz!

'Hawd the game, boys.' We see Rab pointing over at the school with that leery grin on his fat plukey face. 'Look at the lassies up at the window!'

We all crack up laughing. I might have known! Wee Sally Taylor and her mates are swaying with their arms in the air as if they're on the terrace at Rover Park already. I tell you, the whole school is going mental about this cup final. And I'll be going mental with Sally later!

'C'mon, lads,' Lovett says. 'Stop encouraging them.'

Then we see old Wilma the art teacher yelling at the girls and telling them to get away from the window and sit down.

'It's time we were getting back to class as well,' the coach says, turning into a teacher again. 'I've got you for Modern Studies next.'

'C'mon, sur,' Rab says, helping Mr Lovett pile up the parking cones. 'Stay for extra-time.

Play another wee game with us. We'll no' grass ya tae the rector if ya dog the class.'

'*Guthrie*, that's your final warning, boy . . .' But even the coach can't keep a straight face.

'How would you lads feel about some extra football practice at the weekend?' Mr Lovett asks us as we walk back to the changing rooms at the gym. 'I don't mind giving up a Sunday morning. I think it would do you the world of good before the cup final.'

'You bet, sir,' I say. He doesn't have to ask me twice!

The lads break out with laughter.

Well, it's my own fault. I told you I get carried away sometimes. But we're all up for the game – not just me. The team don't mind getting a last-minute practice match in for the big game. Just look at them all nodding at each other and giving the coach the thumbs up sign. That's what I mean about old Lovett – he's brilliant. He's willing to give up his day off for us when he could just as easily be at home watching the Sky Sports channel.

Mr Lovett stops at the school gate. 'So what d'you say, lads? Are we going to win this cup or not?'

'Yessssss, sir!'

We all punch our fists in the air.

'Scotla*aaaaaaaaaaaaaaaaaaaaand*!!!'

It's a guy thing, I'm thinking as I make my way

to Modern Studies, my mind still on the wee male bonding lesson we've just had there with old Love it Lovett. I'm pretty much clued up on all that 'understanding the New Age man' stuff they give you in the women's magazines. I'm not saying I'd run around a male bonding camp-fire at night with Mr Lovett and the lads wearing only Iron John pants and pretending we're Apache Indians. But maybe – who knows? – I might even become best mates with the coach when I leave school. After I slip him and his babe a couple of spare tickets for the stand at Hampden Park when I'm playing for Scotland, I mean. I don't even know if old Love it Lovett has a girlfriend. He's pretty good looking so he probably has his pick of chicks. Probably has to fight them off. Any gorgeous young stunner he wants. Well, I hope he does. It can't be much fun going home to a cold empty sad lad pad after all those extra hours he's been putting in for the team lately.

I'll have to ask Rab if he knows anything about old Lovett's love life. With a name like that, somebody must love him, and I don't just mean his mum.

4

School's out for the day. I was planning to follow Melanie Anderson home again 'cause she lives down my way anyway. Actually, she doesn't really. She lives in those posh houses up the top end of town and I'll have to hare it all the way back to my house before I miss my dinner. Only trouble is, I can't seem to see Mel baby anywhere.

Then I spot wee Sally Taylor standing over by the gate on her own waiting for one of her mates to walk home with. She's already got her blue blazer off and over her bag, school tie loose, creased white blouse wide open at the neck and hanging out over her skirt.

'How's the footballer's legs?' I say for a bit of a wind-up 'cause I know how much she hates having to wear her school uniform. That'll get her back for that mickey-take with her mates at the window when we were playing footie over in the park.

'*How's you-know-who*?' Sally says, smiling.

I give a really false laugh to cover up my red neck and say, 'Almost didn't recognise ya there without the tracksuit and trainers. Yer definitely a girl today.'

'Are you flirting with me, Joey Burns?'

'Get outta here, *uggo*.'

I quickly scan the playground to see if anybody's tuning in. *Phew*, that was a close one!

I tell her, 'Kick-off's at six in my back garden if it doesn't rain. Don't be late, mate.'

Then I beat it, my face on fire all the way down the road.

That night, during the practice session as I run after a stray ball I've hit up the top end of the garden, Sally says, 'Wonder where Dug is? I've not seen him around for the last couple of days.'

Dug's our unofficial team mascot; a wee Jack Russell terrier from down the road who's always gate-crashing the stadium when he sees me and Sally playing with the ball. He's as mad about football as Sally and me are put together. He really is. Sometimes you can't even get the ball off him when he's dribbling up the wing. He's a good ball boy, too; always racing after stray balls for you. He's even got an Ardrossan Rovers strip – he's black and white. He's only about two or something and he still acts like a little puppy sometimes. You know, slobbering all over your face with his tickly wet tongue when you slip on the grass and wind up on your butt. I thought something was wrong when he hadn't turned up for a game the last couple of days. We usually feed him odds and ends, see;

34

any old scraps of meat that are lying around in the fridge. We even gave the daffy Dug this half-frozen hamburger out of the freezer one night; before we got a microwave for defrosting stuff, I mean. He went and swallowed it down in a oner. A *oner*, I tell you. He was *that* starving. He probably thought it was some kind of doggie ice-lolly.

Truth is, his real master doesn't look after him right. He's Hunter the Punter's dog really – our street's nasty neighbour. We all hate Hunter the Punter 'cause he's always giving everybody grief and aggro. On some icy cold winter nights I've watched Dug from the window, tap-dancing away paw-deep in the snow outside under the glow of the lamppost 'cause Hunter the Punter was too lazy to get up out of his king-size Slumberland when he heard Dug scratching at the door. I wanted to sneak the poor wee boy into our house for the night, but my mum would have gone mental if she'd caught me.

Sally and I used to think that Dug was short for Douglas. But it's not. Dug is just Hunter the Punter's sloppy Scottish slang for *dog*. He doesn't even have the decency to give the poor wee boy a name tag.

'He's probably playing away, Sal,' I say with a grin.

'Don't tell me Robbo's dog's in heat *again*?'

'Aye, I'll bet Dug's on guard dog duty

35

outside her house right now, making sure no other mutts make a move on his girlfriend.'

Sally gives me one of her knowing looks. 'Just like boys when they follow girls home from school, huh?'

Hey, that's a bit near the bone here, pal, and it makes me think Sally's rumbled my top secret surveillance operation on Melanie Anderson. That crack about following girls home, and the little dig at school earlier, make me wonder just how much she really does know or suspect about me and you-know-who. Or if anybody else has spotted me shadowing Mel from a safe distance, come to that matter. Right, it's the old FBI Special Agent disguise from now on.

I try to laugh if off. 'He's probably camping outside Mrs Robson's gate right now, hoping to get a glimpse of her golden retriever.'

'Aye,' Sally says, ' and he's not the only boy getting hot under the collar about a golden girl just now. The blonde bitch!'

'*Sally*!'

And then she kicks the ball at me for no reason at all.

5

'You look a bit pale,' my mum says when I get in the house. 'Are you feeling OK, son?'

'Not so hot. I think I'm going down with the flu.' It suddenly just came on me as Sal and I were finishing up the footie training. I feel terrible, so I do. So weak. The week before the big game as well! I'd better be fit for the final.

'Are you sure you're not taking too much out of yourself with that football of yours? You know you've got your school exams coming up again soon.'

'It's probably only a light cold, *Maw*.'

'There's a lot of that Chinese flu going around just now,' she says, suddenly concerned. Aye, and getting ready to mother me with Lemsips as well, I'll bet. Think I don't know the symptoms for a Chinese flu!

'I worry about you, son.'

'I know.'

A natural Florence Nightingale as she squints away at her knitting in the dim living room light. What's that she's ... Naw! I stopped wearing Arran sweaters when I was twelve, Maw! There's just no telling some people, though.

I switch on the overhead lights as she leans forward in her seat and says, 'Go on, then. Get ready for bed and I'll bring you up a hot Lemsip.'

Told ya.

'I'd better take your temperature,' my mum says, small but big, getting to her feet, those eyes of hers that never miss anything still on me. 'Just to be on the safe side . . .' She moves in for the kill like a smiling night nurse with a cold bedpan.

'C'mon, Maw.' I draw back. 'It might be contagious. You might catch it yourself . . . Keep away now . . . You never know . . .'

Every night this week I've been lying awake in bed thinking about my future. What future? I don't even have a job lined up for when I leave school in the summer. What if Ardrossan Rovers don't take me on? What if I don't get discovered by a talent scout at all and I have to get a real job instead? What if my mum makes me stay on for sixth year? What if Melanie leaves and gets a job in the Royal Bank of Scotland and gets off with one of those suit-wearing, pen-pushing posers.

What if?
What if?
What if?
Aaaaaaagh!

All I know is that time is running out if I'm going to score with Melanie. I'll soon be into extra-time with Standard *and* Higher Grades and, before you know it, the whistle's gone and the game's over. I mean once you've done a runner from school that's it – you never see the same crummy crowd again. Everybody starts working and meeting new people and before you know it – hey, Lottery, it could be you! – you've got a brand new life to play with. I'm already worrying about all the older blokes with flash cars and loadsa money that Melanie's bound to meet when she starts working in an office – 'cause that's the kind of job she'll be going after, you know – 'cause she's the brainy type with big plans for the future.

Leave my Mel alone!

My dream of everlasting love dissolves in front of me like one of my alky dad's Alka Selt-zers. I'm a desperate disprin here. Crushed. How am I going to get off with Melanie before it's too late?

I can't even ask my dad for advice now either. He must have been in the same situation as me at one time. He had loads of girlfriends before he married my mum, you know, so she told me. Aye, and a few afterwards as well, her friends told her. He was a lad all right, my dad, in his day. Oh, I still can't believe it . . .

Dead.

Dad.

Dead.

You're not supposed to go until you're a grandpa at least and me and Melanie have got kids of our own. Now you'll never see them growing up to be footballers like me – like you once were. You told me a Burns was born to put the ball in the net. I still remember, Dad, I still remember. Now you'll never see me playing for Ardrossan Rovers like you used to. I wanted you to be so proud of me, Dad, I really did. I thought that playing for the Rovers might have helped you get off the drink. I would have let you train me again like when I was younger; the way we used to play with the ball Brazilian-style on South Beach without any shoes on.

I know you argued with my mum a lot and you never loved each other the way you used to. I know you only stayed together for my sake. And I know I always took my mum's side – but she's my mum. But that didn't mean I didn't love you too, Dad. I'm still your boy. I've got your face, the same right foot as you. It's not fair, it's just not fair. Why did it have to happen to you, why did it have to happen to you?

I loved my dad, you know. I loved him so much, but I never told him. I could never actually bring myself to say the words to his face. You've only got one dad, you know, and my dad was my dad. Oh, Dad, if you can hear me, please believe that. I know you had your problems, your frustrations, your reasons for being the way you were.

But why did you leave me?

That's what I just don't understand!

The police said he must have fallen off the pier sometime after the pub shut, around midnight. I don't know what my dad was doing going for a walk down the harbour at that time of night; it was miles away from our house and the High Tide pub. Maybe he went to re-live the good old days, a sad old man with his memories of the past.

Ardrossan has one of the biggest harbours in Scotland, you know, with ferries running in and out all over the place to the Isle of Arran and everything. They found my dad's body next to where the Arran boat is docked. Face down in the water with all his clothes on. I'm trying not to think about it – how he must have felt. Imagine drowning in that cold dark oily harbour? And around midnight, too, with nobody about. Just the rusty boats creaking against the harbour walls and the spooky old cranes towering above them like giant gravestones marking the great years of the docks that were decades ago.

The water's really dark and deep and scary looking there at night. It must have been freezing too. I'm trying not to think about my dad struggling and panicking in the water 'cause I know how bad a swimmer he was. He probably didn't know what happened to him – with the drink, I mean. That's what the police told my mum when she had to go and identify the body. She was bawling her eyes out – really breaking down mental. I was totally surprised when my gran told me that. Considering how much my parents argued.

They were always fighting; always, always in a ruck over something. The drink made my dad go in bad moods and get angry with my mum for no reason and they'd end up arguing like a pair of crazies. I used to go to my room when they got the boxing gloves out 'cause it used to nip my head in. I'd hear them shouting at each other anyway, even when I had my hands over my ears and my head buried in the pillow. I used to pretend to be asleep when my mum came in later to see if I was all right. She'd corner me in the kitchen the next morning anyway and give me the old forgiveness spiel, 'He's still yer faither, son, no matter what.' Poor Maw, what she must have had to put up with from my dad all those years. And now she's got me to worry about; me at my awkward age.

My mum has built up all these high expectations of me, based on my dad's failings. Her worst nightmare is that I'll end up like him. No way. I want more than a faded football shirt that doesn't fit any more.

6

I'm sitting in the living room, watching one of my fave 'chick-flick' vids and it's not even lunchtime yet, when the door bell starts buzzing. I was just getting to the good bit as well where this blonde babe is dancing on top of a bar room table and she's wearing this sexy napkin-size mini skirt. She's got these gorgeous cheerleader legs that go all the way up to her chin and I was, like, you know, just about to dive to the floor with my finger on the old remote control pause button so that I could sneak a better look up her skirt; just to check out what colour pants she's got on, if you must know. Will they be black this time, will they be white? Weh hey! Woh ho! I mean you can't even see anything. Not really. No matter how much you crane your stupid crazy neck up against the TV screen.

I press the mute button and dive for the door.

'*Sally*!' I'm totally gobsmacked. 'What are *you* doing here?'

'Sorry to disturb you . . . I was just wondering if you've got over your flu yet?'

'Aye, almost. I'm just a bit blocked up. My

head's a little fuzzy still. You're lucky you caught me in, Sal. I was just on my way up the shops to get some messages for my maw.'

'*In your bathrobe?*'

Oh aye, I forgot to mention that. I've still got on this old blue bathrobe I usually wear when I'm hanging around the house on Sunday mornings; or when I'm off school sick, like today. To tell you the truth, I'm glad Sally's dropped by. I was getting bored to bits with my maw phoning me up from the chip shop where she works every five minutes with that worried voice of hers and asking how I'm feeling and if I've taken my Lemsip fix yet. Sally's probably worried as well; in case I won't be fit enough for the cup final. I've been worried sick, too. Two days off school and no football training!

'Were you still in bed?' Sally asks.

'Naw, just watchin' telly.'

'Are you sure you're OK? You're acting *weird.*'

'I toleja . . . I'm feeling a lot better. I'll probably be back at school tomorrow. I'm – hey, what about you? Why aren't *you* in school?'

'I've plunked it.'

'*You've what?*' I look at her, puzzled.

'I'm doggin' school.'

'Did yer hairdryer melt yer brain this morning? You'll get detention if they catch you.' I have a quick Neighbourhood Watch up and down the street. 'C'mon, get in the house before an informer grasses you to the Gestapo.'

Sally plonks down on the sofa and pulls out
the video box I've hidden behind the crochet
cushions. Crochet cushions, I ask you! She
stares at the homemade video sleeve plastered
with pics of that sexy babe I was just telling you
about and a mile of yellowing Sellotape.

'Yer not watching *her* again?' she slags me off.
'Still pretending she's Melanie Anderson, eh?'

I grab the box off her. 'Didja want me to
forge a sick letter for ya, is that it?'

'Naw.' She shakes her head, all serious now.
'It's Dug. He got picked up by the dog van.
They've got him down the pound.'

'Are you sure?'

'Aye, I heard Mrs Murphy talkin' at the bus
stop on my way to school. She said they
huckled him last Friday. Last Friday, Joey!
That's why he's been doggin' the football
training. I've been in torture all morning
worrying about him.'

'Have you told Hunter the Punter?'

Sally pulls a fake scary face and covers her
mug with a cushion as if she's watching some
spoof horror movie. 'I'm not goin' to that
psycho's house. No way. He gives me the creeps
just seeing him in the street. Y'know he doesn't
care about Dug. Why d'you think he hasn't
gone for him himself.' She looks at me long and
hard. 'Will you go with me to the dog pound,
Joey?'

It's not that I don't *want* to go, but . . . 'You mean right now?'

Sally doesn't answer me but her eyes are saying everything. Hey, there's no need to twist my arm here. I'll go, I'll go.

'Where is it?' I ask her.

'Dunno. Stevenston, I think.'

'Well that's a big help.' A sudden thought comes to me. 'I'll get on the blower to the council and find out the right address. No point in tearin' all the way out to Stevenston for nowt.' I head for the hall phone, stop for a second, then carry on up the stairs. 'Let me get changed first,' I call down. 'Won't be a minute.'

'Hurry up, Joey. They might've put him to sleep already.'

'Yer not wearing *that* T-shirt,' Sally tells me when I storm down the stairs, ready for action. She's always telling me what *not* to wear.

'Whadaya mean? It's a Tommy Hilfiger copy,' I coolly mention in my best impress-yer-friend voice. 'The authentic article: a genuine, hundred percent black market forgery. Rab Guthrie's sister bought it for me at a rip-off stall in Ibiza.'

'I don't care where Tracy Guthrie buys her tacky tourist gifts – or gets them out for the lads. It doesn't go with those checked trousers.'

'They're both blue and white. Scotland colours.'

That should win her over.

46

'Stripes don't go with checks,' she says again, only louder. 'Go and put jeans on, then, if you want.'

If *I* want? I look at Sally as I slowly count to ten . . . *Not*! 'Ya'd think we were going on a date or something.'

'With *you*, Joey Burns? You wish, pal.' She sighs. 'Boys just don't have a clue about clothes . . .'

I'm digging the World War Three trench right here. 'Well *your* new Reebok trainers don't exactly go with yer school uniform.'

'It's a long hike to Stevenston, y'know.' She starts staring me out – her hands on her hips now with the old 'make-me-or-take-me' Girl Power stance. 'I'm being practical, pal, that's a big difference.'

Girls really get me sometimes – the way they've got these handy pocket-size answer books for everything. I mean, lads just throw anything on – but girls! They can take all night to get ready! Rab Guthrie picked this chick up at her pad once on a hot date and he ended up sitting there for three hours getting grilled by her parents while the chick was getting babed-up in the bathroom. And she wasn't even gorgeous looking either.

I mean *come on*. We're supposed to be dealing with a life-threatening emergency situation here – rushing to save poor Dug from being put down. Do you think that when the old SAS have to rescue hostages from a hijacked Boeing

47

747 or abseil into a besieged embassy building, they've got time to stop and wonder to themselves: Hmmmn, will I wear that stripey Gaultier sweater again or will I slip on that nice new Ralph Lauren polo neck? Do they *Bravo Two Zero* as like! The SAS bods just throw on any old black jumpers and trousers that are hanging up in their wardrobes and then that's them – *tango, tango!* – away in the helicopter!

And we're not even taking the bus!

'Yer not going out with me dressed like that, Joey Burns, and that's final. Go back and get changed, now.'

7

At the dog pound, in this deserted industrial section of Stevenston, two towns away, the gates are unlocked but we can't see the warden anywhere. Great. So it looks as if he's on his lunch break.

Sally and I are standing outside gazing up at this rundown, dirty, whitewashed building with hundreds of brown doors that looks as if it might have been horse stables at one time, and Sally's got my arm clamped and is pushing me forward as I try to do a slow motion action replay in reverse, my legs wobbling.

'Go on, Joey. You go first. They won't have guard dogs.'

If Sally's so sure why doesn't *she* go first.

'Go on . . .' She gives me another shove. 'What'ya waiting for?'

'I've seen the horror movie, Sal. I know what happens when you step through the gates.'

'I'm telling ya, there are *no* dogs.'

There are dogs.

Two of them.

Alsatians.

Big and vicious looking. Barking their rabid heads off as they come charging towards us.

'Run!'

Check us out, ya nosey Neighbourhood Watch grasser! We're sitting on the wall of this Budget Van Hire building across the road from the dog pound, wondering whether to phone Sally's detective dad up at the cop shop and worrying if old CID-serious sarge will chuck his fugitive daughter behind bars for pulling a big school break-out. He probably would as well – he's *that* serious. One of those big silent types who never say anything but never miss a thing, if you know what I mean. Trying to act like a regular guy but secretly sizing you up and making you feel as if you've stolen something or broken some crummy outdated law. He probably carries a spare pair of handcuffs with him when he goes for the weekly shop in Safeways – just in case he has to make a quick off-duty citizen's arrest.

Don't get me wrong. It's not that I don't like Sally's dad. It's him who doesn't like *me*. He probably thinks I'm a bad influence on his precious daughter. Probably blames me for turning daddy's girl into a football-mad tomboy. Same as that time he blamed me for getting Sally hooked on Action Man instead of Barbie when she was just a tiny little kid.

To be honest, though, I don't really know Sally's dad that well; 'cause he's never *there* to get to know. Her mum's pure magic and you couldn't wish for better neighbours, but old Serious Sarge is always away working on some police case. And whenever he's at home, he's always on *my* case for accidentally kicking the ball over the fence into his poxy rose garden!

A couple of minutes later, I sneak another quick peek at Sally while she's glancing at her sporty Swatch watch again. She's been silent for a while now, and I know it's not that slab of flu-friendly butt-cold concrete we're sitting on that's causing the big chill with her laddish chit-chat. I can tell she wants to talk about something and I only hope it's not about my dad. I know Sally means well and she's only trying to let me know that she's there for me, but I'm just not ready to talk about it yet. I mean, it's hard not to want to talk about it 'cause it's all I can think about just now.

I think about my dad, dead six weeks now, and it's as if he's still here. I mean some of his things are still in his room the way he left them. My mum's been so busy putting in all those extra hours at the chippie to pay for the funeral that we haven't had a chance to ship it all down to the charity shop yet. The funny thing is, my dad's razor was still clogged up with his thick grey-black bristles when my mum was clearing out the bathroom cabinet and putting his stuff in black polybags for the bin. So what I did was, I pinched it and stuck it in my bottom drawer where I keep all my football programmes and the pile of letters from this girl called Linda Faulkner who was mad about me once.

Good old Linda wasn't drop-dead gorgeous looking or anything like Melanie Anderson is, but I liked hanging around with her anyway. She was into the Scripture's Union in a big way at school and I joined up just to pray around with her. You should have heard me singing those hippy trippy tunes old Wilma Rubber Fingers, our arty art teacher, can strum away on her battered old acoustic guitar. I was so bad at singing, they let me do a rap so I wouldn't have a poxy inferiority complex or anything. Bless them. But I stopped shaking the tambourine with the old Born-Again bunch when Linda went on a pilgrimage up to Inverurie after her dad got a job on the North Sea oil rigs. It wasn't that long afterwards that she stopped sending me those pukey pink envelopes which reeked of Exclamation perfume. I suppose old Linda must be mad about some other lad now. You get used to people leaving you after a while anyway.

It's not until a van pulls up outside the Budget rental office and we shuffle along the wall a bit to the DIY centre next door that Sally finally says, 'There's something I've been meaning to tell you.'

Here we go . . .

'Is it about my dad?'

'Well no, not really. But if you feel like talking about him, I'm all ears.'

I smile at her. 'Yer a regular wee Samaritan.'

Sally isn't smiling.

'Listen, Joey, I don't know how to tell you. So I'm just going to tell you.'

'Tell me what?'

And even before she speaks, I know what she's going to say.

'I think Melanie Anderson's seeing someone else.'

My heart sinks. 'Are – are you sure?'

'Sorry.'

'Ya could at least lie a little and say yer not certain . . . Can't you see I'm dying here.'

'Sorry, Joey.'

I'm dying all right . . . to kill someone! I can't believe it! Two days off school and already Melanie's doing the dirty on me. Two poxy days!

'Who's the lucky lad?' I ask, all calm, all composed . . . like, *right*. 'I'm gonna kill the creep! I'm gonna kill him! Hold me back, Sal. Hold me back! *Who is it*?'

'William Climie.'

'*Slimey Climie*? Are you serious?'

'Very.'

'Slimey Climie from sixth year? He's got his own car and everything.'

'I know, he's practically a man.'

'Go on, why don'tcha put another bullet in my head just to make sure I'm dead.'

'Sorry.'

'*Willya stop saying sorry!*'

'Sorry.'

Half an hour later, we're still hanging around outside the dog pound, and I'm ready to beat it back to my place. I wish I'd never come now. I wish I'd never taken the poxy days off school. Two poxy days!

Slimey Climie.

That big sweaty jockstrap!

It wouldn't be so bad if Slimey Climie was in the school Debating Society or the Young Ornithologists' Club – but he's the scrummy wummy captain of the school rugby team, for godsakes! He isn't just practically a man like Sally says . . . he's practically a walking male model!

Oh, Melanie, how could you have done this to me? After all the big plans I've made for us.

Just look what happens when you take a couple of days off school.

Two poxy days!

Just as Sally and I are about to nip into the nearest phone box and call up police reinforcements, we see the lunch crowd spilling out of the pub down the road and this old grey-haired warden geezer dressed in dirty dungarees, heading for the dog pound.

'We're looking for a wee Jack Russell,' Sally

says, catching up with the grumpy grandpa at the gate. 'His name's Dug.'

'I've got loads of dugs,' the old codger chortles when he's tied up his Nazi guard dogs. 'None of them with name tags or collars. That's why they get picked up as strays.'

'He's black and white,' Sally persists, sweeping a strand of dark hair from her pale, worried face.

'So's a Dalmatian, hen. Aye, an' I've probably had a hundred and one of them over the years, tae!'

Ho, ho . . . Hem, hem! You've really got me in hysterics here, Grandpa.

Finally, I say, 'Couldja just look and see if he's there, pal.'

So we walk across the courtyard and watch the old crumbly opening up these tall, narrow doors where they must have kept the horses originally. He's not a happy chappy, I can tell you, our trying-hard-to-stand-up-pub-comedian-grandpa. There must be twenty doors at least, the paint peeling and flaking all over the place, and the old codger's getting well narked at having to give us the old musty museum guided tour routine. It's dead dark and damp and dismal inside the prison cells, and the pong! Sprinkle some Shake 'n' Vac, Grandpa, *purlease*! All these poor dogs with desperate faces, just lying there in beds of stale straw that must have been left over from the first cereal advert in 1886. And still the old geezer's opening doors.

Pit Bull Terrier.

Labrador.

Doberman.

'*Dug!*' Sally screams.

Dug jumps up suddenly like a substitute in the last five minutes of the FA cup final, his tail wagging like crazy.

'Gimme a paw,' Sally says.

'Gimme a fiver,' the old geezer says.

'Gimme a break,' I say. '*What for?*'

The old geezer goes, 'What d'you think this is – a free hostel for the homeless? Somebody has to feed the mutts, y'know. That'll be five pounds, please, cheques made payable to the pound.'

8

Even though Sally and I ring the door bell like a drug squad raid by the rozzers, it still takes Hunter the Punter about ten hours to open his front door. As he unbolts his dungeon and the door creaks eerily open, we're greeted by this stale greasy smell wafting out from somewhere. I can't specifically say it's the kitchen; it's a general, all-round stink as if someone's lobbed a can of tear gas through the broken front window that's partly-covered with peeling Sellotape.

Then he finally appears: the phantom of the rock opera himself, wearing a grimy-grey Harley-Davidson T-shirt splattered with a year's supply of pukey food stains; the straggly heavy metal hairdo tumbling to his shoulders, as black as his manky blue jeans. Hunter the Punter gives me the serial killer creeps. He's a real bogeyman. Look! The spook's got his finger right up there trying to worm a big greenie out of his nose like a whelk from a shell. Nobody's got a nastier neighbour than us. No wonder Dug's cowering behind Sally. He doesn't want to go 'home' either. I glance over at Sally whose . . . Hang on a minute there, buddy-buddy sidekick! Where's my S.W.A.T. team backup? She's sneaking back down the path with Dug in her arms, the partners in pranks sniggering away like Dick Dastardly and Muttley!

'Whadaya want, son?' a voice bellows out from behind me.

No: 'Hello, there. How can I help you?' Just straight out with the pump-action shotgun.

I turn round, trembling. 'I've brought your dog back, Mr Hunter.'

'Why, has he been away on holiday somewhere?'

'He got huckled by the dog van,' Sally calls out from behind the hedge.

Hunter the Punter squints in Sally's direction, straining his peepers to make her out through the overgrown jungle camouflage. All of a sudden, he coughs up some phlegm, swallows it and breathes his pukey ashtray-breath all over me. 'Is that right noo. And there's me thinkin' some bugger had nicked him.'

'It cost me five quid to get him out,' I mention, then I show him the receipt which I was clever enough to keep. 'I had to pay for four days' food.'

'*Four days*? The greedy wee bugger! One tin of Kenomeat lasts him all week in ma hoose.'

'It was my mum's money for the messages, y'know. She'll go mental when I tell her.' Aye,

58

she'll be going mental all right. And if I don't get the dosh back it'll be me who'll be getting put down next.

'A fiver? Yur maw's money ya say?' He scratches his sandpaper stubble with a claw of dirty black fingernails. 'Look, son, I'm a bit skint at the moment. Tellya what, why don'tcha just keep the bloody dug? He's too much bother for me anyway. Always sneakin' off somewhere . . . ya wee bugger, yeh! Don't think I can't see ya hidin' behind that hedge!'

Aye, and who can blame him.

Sally looks at me as I say, 'Can you take him?' though I know exactly what her answer's going to be.

'Y'know I'm not allowed to have any pets in our house, Joey.'

'Oh, aye, I forgot your dad's allergic to animals,' I say. I say it in this very understanding voice so that she'll understand just exactly what it is I'm thinking: does that include big cuddly wuddly Police dogs as well, Serious Sarge?

Then, without any air raid warning, Hunter the Punter drops a 'smart' bomb on me that sends me two steps back as I climb into my germ warfare suit and clamp my gas mask over my mug. If the fallout from his fart attacks ever leak out, we'll have the old NATO weapon inspectors over here.

'D'ya want him or no', son? Ma Crispy Mince Pancakes will be burnt tae a crisp in a minute.' He swings round. 'Can ya no' smell that smoke!'

Aye, and that's not the only outbreak of Ebola my radiation detector's picking up, ya dirty big caring pet-lover!

'I'll take him, I'll take him,' I say in this really excited voice as if I'm snapping up a discount bargain from the guy with the microphone at Saltcoats market.

'Now bugger off, you two, and let me get back tae ma grub!'

And with that parting shot, Hunter the Punter turns, dropping another smart fart on me as he slams the door shut behind his smoke screen retreat.

'Come on, Dug,' I say as I take him off Sally, trying to cover both our noses, and carry him across the road to my house. 'You might not be a free transfer, boy, but you're joining the home team.'

'Yeah! Way to go, Joey!' Sally starts skipping and jumping all over the street as she punches her fist in the air like a jammy Lottery winner on the way to the nearest car showroom. Even wee Dug's cocking his head to one side as he looks at her in confusion. Sally still acts like a little puppy dog herself when she gets excited. I'm not kidding. Girls. They really crack me up sometimes. But in a nice way.

9

Back home in my kitchen, I'm defrosting a steak for Dug in the microwave when I suddenly say to him, 'Your name's Laddie now.'

'*Laddie*?' Sally repeats.

I laugh. 'Well, Rover is a bit obvious.'

'The black-and-white Ardrossan Rovers strip, huh?' Sally beams at me as she bends over and claps the wee boy. 'He's one of the lads now, all right.'

'It's more than that, Sal . . .' I lean down and stroke the wee boy's head as he licks his chops in anticipation of the posh grub I'm about to serve up for him. 'Every dog deserves a name . . . and a home with free food.'

'Oh, Joey Burns . . . you're the best.'

I look at Sally for a long time, then I say, really meaning it as well, 'I couldn't do anything about my dad dying, but I had the chance to save Dug. I mean Laddie . . .'

The wee boy barks and whimpers, dancing up and down on the linoleum, his tiny stump of a tail wagging like crazy. 'See, he likes his new name!' I bend over and stroke him again. 'He's got the chance of a new life now,' I say, gazing up into Sally's eyes as she beams away at me. 'He can be your dog as well, Sal, even if he stays here with me. I just hope my maw doesn't go mental when she sees him.'

'We can both take turns with the walkies, if ya want.'

Sally's getting all gushy now as she goes to hug me one. Girls have a habit of doing that to you, you know, if you're a bit of a hero. It happens all the time in the movies.

'I'm so proud of—'

Saved by the bell!

I swiftly dodge the tackle as I reach for the microwave. 'C'mon, Sal, the timer's buzzing. The steak'll be ruined. *Quick*, pass me a plate . . .'

'Ya know what?' Sally says as we watch Laddie running after the ball in my back garden. 'Boys are just like dogs sometimes.'

Boy, she sure knows how to make a guy feel gorgeous.

'Thanks for the compliment.'

'No, I don't mean looks. Well, maybe some boys, like Rab Guthrie. He's got a tongue like a Labrador when he sees girls. And he smells like a wet dog too sometimes.' She giggles. 'No, what I mean is boys follow you around like dogs when they like you.'

Hah! So she *has* found out about me and Melanie Anderson. Time for a quick deflection here, before she starts commentating on that little out-of-school game I've been playing.

'Are boys following you around now?' I ask, hitting the ball back to the goalkeeper.

'That's for me to know and you to find out.'

I've got her on the defensive now.

'I'm intrigued . . . Go on, Sal, tell me more. How else are boys like dogs?'

'Well,' she says, lifting Laddie up in her arms. 'Boys like to put on this big butch macho act, but underneath we know yer just big softies who love to be cuddled.'

'I don't know if I'd go that far.' Well, maybe with Melanie Anderson. I might even lick her all over; on the nose and in her ears and everything.

'Good boy!' Sally drops Laddie on the grass. 'Ball, go get the ball.'

'You've got the ball boy well trained.'

'Ya just have to shout, "run", and dogs fetch anything,' she says, grinning. 'And guess what? Boys are just the same.'

'Woof! Woof!' Laddie barks.

I laugh. 'Y'know, Sal, I think *you* look like a dog sometimes.'

Suddenly, without even whispering, 'Seconds out!', Sally smacks me in the stomach with her fist. Wow! What a knock-out punch! I double over in agony from the killer blow, struggling to get to my feet before the ref counts to ten. If you don't think wee Sally 'Knuckles'

Taylor can hit like a champ, you're betting on the wrong boxer!

'C'mon, Sal, calm down. I don't mean looks. I mean the way you *look* at *me* sometimes.'

Sally looks at me, another right hook at the ready. 'What way?'

I grin. 'With yer big brown puppy-dog eyes.'

She pushes me away. 'Are you winding me up, pal?'

'Naw, I like it.' I really do. I swear. That's the crazy punch-drunk thing about it all.

'In what way d'ya like it?' Sally's big puppy browns are on me now all right.

'I don't know what way,' I say. I don't either. I just know, that's all. How else are you supposed to answer that kind of stupid question? The kind of stupid question girls are always hitting you with! 'All I know is that I like it. It's kind of, I don't know, cute.'

'*Cute*? What kind of crummy word is that to use!' Sally has her hand on her mouth and she's giggling away, all girlishly, and I know she likes what I've told her; even though she's pretending she doesn't. I don't even know why she likes it. I don't even know why I said it, to be honest. I mean, I meant what I said, but I didn't exactly mean it the way it came out; in those exact words, I mean. I love it when Sally goes loopier-than-loopy for no reason. I don't know why I do, but I do. It kills me when girls are cute.

64

My mum's straight up to high doh when she gets home from the chippie. Doh, ray, me, fah, soh, lah, tee . . . DOH!

'What d'you mean you never got my milk and bread?' She hangs up that old washed-out work anorak of hers in the kitchen cupboard then pulls open the freezer door. 'Did you at least get the—Where's the steak for your dinner?'

Ooops! I think she's spotted the cellophane wrapper sticking out of the bin.

'What's going on, Joey?'

'Oh aye, I was just going to tellya . . .'

So I tell her how Sally and I saved Laddie from being put down and how Hunter the Punter said I could keep him 'cause he didn't have a fiver to pay me back. Well *technically* me, but my maw to be more *precise*. See, that's the kind of point she never fails to remind me of, my maw.

'I cook and clean in that chip shop five days a week. And I've got a hoose to keep as well. And you're throwing the money away. Throwing it away! You're just like yer faither, Joey Burns, and y'know what happened to him!'

I'm still trying to get over him dying as well, you know. I don't need the constant reminder. It's in my mind all the time. All the time.

'A dog'll be no trouble, Maw. Honest. He can sleep in my room with me. Or my dad's – I mean, the spare room . . .'

'I wish yer faither was here now,' she says

wearily. 'He'd know what to do with you.' She slumps down on the stool, her head in her hands, sobbing softly. ''Cause I just don't know any more, son . . .'

'You don't have to worry about me, Maw.'

Now *isn't* a good time, Joey . . .

'Er, Maw . . . ' I grab a cloth from the sink and start wiping the mess I made on the table when I was feeding Laddie. 'Ya couldn't lend me another couple of quid, couldja . . .?'

'*What*?' She blinks at me, her eyes all bleary. '*What for now*?'

'Well, I have to buy Laddie a dog tag now that he's got a name . . . and, er, uhm, a wee collar and lead. Y'know, Maw, one of those tartan ones to prove he supports Scotland . . .'

Boy, is she up off that stool and in my face again!

'D'you think I've got another wee part-time night job going in the Clydesdale Bank or something? Dear God,' she adds and subtracts and multiplies, her mind ringing up the cash register right in front of me again. 'Next there'll be vet's bills and . . .' She scurries through to the living room and I'm hot on her heels like a defender chasing a star striker who's just broken through the offside trap. We both look at Laddie, lying on the green carpet in front of the gas fire; his new pitch now; his bulging gut full of prime beef steak, fast asleep.

Then, all of a sudden, he gives a wee

high-pitched doggie howl as if he's barking in his sleep.

'He must be having a dream,' my mum says.

'More like a nightmare where he's just been,' I tell her. And I don't mean the dog pound either.

'To tell you the truth, son, I've always felt sorry for that wee Dug.'

'His name's Laddie *noo*!'

'Aye, and who's going to look after him tomorrow when you're at school and I'm down the chip shoop'

Uh oh. She's moving in on me again – there's just no stopping her! Time to sneak out the back door Maw Exit again.

'Is he at least house trained, son?'

'Me and Sally trained him ourselves. He's in the home team. He's our official team mascot now.'

'I give up, son.'

10

First day back at school after being off sick. Only I'm still sick. Sick to the stomach, that is.

Slimey Climie.

I still can't believe it. When did all this happen? And behind my back as well! Well I'm going to find out. I'm going to make it my mission in life to get to the bottom of this. And before lunch time, too!

It's actually not until lunch time that I catch Melanie Anderson in a clinch with old Slimeball as I come out of the school dining hall with Rab Guthrie. Except they're not exactly sharing saliva here – or even having some kissy wissy love chat either. More like a massive bust-up, if you ask me. But let's ask Rab Guthrie, anyway, just to be certain . . .

I turn to Rab. 'Wonder what's going on?'

'Don't know, mate. William Climie, eh?'

'It doesn't mean they're going out with each other.'

'Well it sure looks that way to me.'

And talking about looks: Slimey Climie looks well over six feet tall, now that I've had a chance to size him up in the flesh. Slimey Climie with his male model looks and his wavy black hair and sideburns. He's a real quick-growth man with that day-old stubble on his Armani-man chin. I'll bet he polishes those shiny brown leather-soled shoes of his with the old Vidal Sasson power pump hairspray for added shine and bounce, too. Basically he's one of those handsome heart-throbs who is more in love with himself than any babe who has the privilege of dating him.

'Oooh, he's sooo gorgeous,' I say in this very gushy schoolgirl's voice.

'Aye,' Rab says, 'he looks like a real jerk.'

I'm getting all territorial here. Hands off my girl, pal! I would never manhandle a lady that way and there's no way a chick like Mel would ever take that kind of strong arm treatment from a smoothie like Slimey. And it's not just verbal abuse either. Supermodel-slinky Melanie's giving as good as she gets and trying to stand her ground. But that hulkin' big hunk has practically got her in a half-nelson wrestling hold.

'C'mon,' I say. 'Let's jump in and help her out.'

As we move over to muscle in with the old wrestling tag match routine, our football coach Mr Lovett bounds over and breaks up the ruck.

'We were only having a wee tiff, sir,' Melanie says in this soft singing voice of hers that would make the Sash sound like a choirboy hymn on the terraces of Ibrox.

'He's not even a real teacher,' Slimey says suddenly. 'He's nothing more than a work experience student.'

Lovett takes a deep breath. 'I don't want to report you now, William.'

'It's OK, sir.' Melanie smiles, embarrassed. 'It was nothing serious.'

'Well, if you're sure . . .' Lovett appears to hesitate, then he says in his best teacher's voice, 'Just remember, William, that Melanie doesn't play quarterback for the All Blacks.'

'Yes, *sir*,' Slimey says through gritted teeth.

For a second it looks as if Slimeball's going to smack old Lovett one in the kisser, but he suddenly steps back, knowing he'd be in BIG trouble if he did, and stomps away to his waiting rugby club mates. See you in detention later, pal. Serves him right, the big creep!

As if on cue, Melanie's cliquey gal pals move in, crowding round her, all girlie whispers of comfort, the defence barricade complete now.

I grin at Rab. 'Don'tcha just love it.'

Not only has good old Love it Lovett taken the team all the way to the cup final – he's now officially my favourite teacher after rushing to the rescue of my Mel. Worra guy!

I can't believe it! Just seconds later, we catch that other ace guy Slimey Climie in a love match with Sarah Maloney behind the tennis courts. He's practically stuck to her like Superglue, testing the old Listerine on her, I'll bet, as they play a game of tonsil tennis together.

What a Slimeball! Aye, well just wait, mate, till Melanie Anderson finds out what a guilty conscience her gorgeous faithful boyfriend has.

It's not until later that afternoon, when I'm on my way over to long jump practice in the park with the rest of my class, that I find out the full plot twist; when I see Slimey Climie laughing and joking with all his rugby team jockstraps at the entrance to the gym, I mean. So I hang back a bit to hear what they're in hysterics about. Obviously he's telling them the latest score: Two Trys to me, lads, eh? Aye, I'm a scrum and a half all right! Just look at that smug, punch-me mug everybody loves (to hate). What a bunch of comedians!

Rugby club humour makes me want to puke up into an empty rugby boot so that I don't stink out their sweaty talcum-powdered changing room, to tell you the truth; those big-muscled weightlifter types back-slapping each other and telling crude, rude jokes that are just a load of crap. I mean, there's dirty jokes and there's dirty jokes, but their kind of toilet humour needs a good dollop of Domestos (i.e. kills all known germs).

I move closer to listen to their conversation, pretending to look at the Wear Bright Gear In Winter poster that's still stuck to the notice-board with brickhard BLU-TACK.

'She's just a spare tyre,' Slimey Climie's bragging away.

'Handy to have if you ever need to change a flat,' one of 'the lads' laughs.

'Aye, she's got Pirelli class all right,' another lad laughs. 'Not like her mate Lucy Harper. Or should I say . . . *Mrs Michelin*!'

Then they all laugh.

The sexy, sweaty jockstraps!

'What am I gonna do?' I ask Sally when I manage to drag her away from her mates during a break in her class shot put practice over in the park. I'm that desperate for help now, I don't care who sees me talking with her.

'It's none of your business,' Sally whispers. 'You can't get involved.'

'It *is* my business. It's my future we're talking about here.'

'Face it, Joey, you don't *have* a future with Melanie Anderson.'

'No, don't say that. Don't—'

'Drop the sad lad act right now, Joey Burns, or I'm outta here! And ya can beat it right back to yer own class, for all I care. Your teacher's watching us, and so is mine.'

Aye, and so are some of my mates as well. I look over to the rest of my class still long jumping at the end of the field.

'Lighten up,' Sally says. 'Let it go.' She suddenly laughs, all matey again. 'Ya big girl's blouse!'

72

She's right, of course. But I'm not giving up without a fight! This is the girl of my dreams we're talking about here. The chick who does the trick for me!

'Listen, Sal . . . ya couldn't give me some more advice, couldja?'

'Ah, the sad lad finally sees sense. So ya want me to coach you on snogging and pulling techniques. From an experienced girl's point of view, of course. From a kid who may or may not have fancied someone before. Go on, *grovel*.'

'I'm grovelling, I'm grovelling. Look, I'm on my knees. Bail me out, buddy. Go on, goalie . . .'

Sally gets to her feet. 'Teach is looking over again. I'd better take a hike.'

And then she's walking away.

I shout, 'I'll see ya tonight!'

'Oh, you'll see me all right,' Sally calls back. 'And sooner than ya think.'

As I wander back across the grass to my own class, grinning and wondering what old Mystic Sal's cryptic comment was about, I see her out the corner of my eye lobbing the shot put into the sand. Then she's jumping up and down and flexing her muscles at her mates 'cause it looks as if she's beaten the school record again.

11

I hate getting detention! Aye, and just wait till my mum finds out later; when I give her that grounded-again-letter from my teacher. I don't know how to tell my mum 'cause she'll go mental. What happened? Erm, well, I nearly got suspended from school for writing this *Boy's Own* story that got banned (well torn into pieces, to be more accurate). It was supposed to be for the school newspaper, the *School Voice*. (The *School Voice*, I ask you!) You know, that wee scandalrag our enthusiastic football coach Love it Lovett got going (except it's not!). So I was going to suggest to the Editor that they spice things up a bit by starting a fiction page, and then I'd submit the story. Not only was I planning to become a regular contributor on the rag, I thought I might impress Melanie Anderson 'cause she's the Features Editor.

Only thing is, the story was more like the kind you get in the lads' mags: dead raunchy and that with loads of the laddish humour we like. A bit of a cringer, I'll admit. For the school paper, I mean. But even Rab Guthrie liked my raunchy wee read. He even tried to help me out by roping this practising Picasso-wannabe who lives up his way into scribbling down the illustrations for free.

Unfortunately, old Wilma Rubber Fingers wasn't laughing when she caught Rab with it in art class, yanked the pages out of his hands, then huckled both our butts. Aye, and you've guessed it: the story had my name at the top of the page – so that's why we both got detention! And even though Wilma said the artwork was really good!

So now I'm serving time for my crime. I'm just on my way to the slammer now, actually. Just one night behind bars and then ... FREEDOM! Dead man walking away! I can take my punishment like a man. Can't wait (except I can!). Oh how I hate evening detention. They make you sit there with all the school hardmen till you're almost cooking a curry in your pants. They're real nasty pasties, the hardmen at our school. Always getting detention for vandalism and beating up nerds and bad-mouthing teachers. And that's where I'm going now.

He*eeeeeeeeeeeeeeeeee*lp!

The old vindaloo-inducing detention room is already packed out when I flash my VIP card to get into the 'strictly members only' club. As I look around for a spare toilet seat to park my butt, my heart suddenly explodes out of my chest. Wee Sally Taylor's sitting up the back of the class, right among the hardmen. Although she's not exactly with them, more like surrounded by them. The hardmen with their you-stare-at-me-again-and-I'll-kick-yer-coupon-in scowls on their ug-thug mugs, their cool, grime-shiny denim uniforms stinking like ashtrays. The look on Sally's face has got nothing to do with that hard wooden seat she's squirming uncomfortably in – wishing she was somewhere else right now, I'm sure, rather than the Babysitters' Club she's mistakenly gate-crashed.

'What are *you* doing here?' I say, moving up the aisle toward the spare seat at her desk.

'I got caught doggin' it.'

'Told ya, didn't I?'

'Aye, maybe you should have forged that sick note for me after all.'

Predictably, someone sticks his leg out in front of me, and he's not trying to trip me up either. Hey . . . what's Slimey Climie doing here? And with some of his rugby scrum as well! Aye, well it serves him right for man-handling my Mel in the playground. Old Lovett should have suspended him from school, if you ask me. Hmmmn, wonder what the password is today to get past his desk?

Creep.

Cretin.

Moron.

Your Majesty.

I don't say anything. Instead I stand my ground, trying to look tough. Obviously I

76

haven't perfected the old hardman pose yet, 'cause the rugby scrum bag with the thick neck and shoulders bulging out of his school blazer is just about to nut me one.

'What are you talking to the geeky girl for?' he wants to know. 'Haven't you seen her out of school? She thinks she's a lad in that tracksuit of hers.' And the punchline is: 'But she's a girl, isn't she? So that means she must be a lezzy, then.'

'Haw, haw!' Sally chortles. 'That was hilarious, ass-face. Y'know, if I was you I'd pull my trousers on over my head and do a handstand with a baseball cap on my bare ass. Nobody would even notice the difference.'

Has she got Mad Cow, or what? She'd better watch out. She won't be splitting her sides in a minute – more like her head open any second.

Slimey's laughing, though. 'Listen to the lassie. I'm shaking in my shoes here.' He stands up slowly, all show. He's not laughing now.

The hardmen posse starts shouting and banging on desks, egging the smug thug on. The rugby scrum are grinning away with the supporters on their side.

'*Smack her one in the kisser, Climie!*'

Slimey Climie holds a hand up as Sally shrinks in her seat. 'See, that's what's wrong with football, Burns.' He turns on me. 'Lassies like her are playing now 'cause everyone knows it's a girls' game.' He moves in on Sally. 'I'll show this clever little lezzy what it means to be

77

a real lad. She's getting the rugby drop-kick now . . .'

That does it! I can't take any more. I'm ready to explode!

I'm thinking: *Just you touch her, pal, and I'll kill ya!*

'What did you just say, Burns?' Slimey's suddenly in my face, his hands clawing at my collar.

Ooops! I must have spoken aloud. Me and my big gob again! Oh, help . . .

'You're dead, Burns. Think you're funny, eh? Now you're really going to be in stitches. You're getting a face-lift, pretty boy.'

Grinning to themselves, the scrum and the posse are up and out of their seats, crowding round us for a playground fistfight. Only we're indoors and one of the hardmen is at the door, holding it shut. I'm trapped in the room, nowhere to run. Ready to serve up the old boil-in-a-bag Beef Madras in my shorts any second now.

'Kill him, Climie,' one of the scrum says fiercely.

'Kick his coupon in!' another one snarls.

'Leave him alone,' Sally squeals, wriggling to get out of the arm-lock two scrum bags have on her at the back of the class.

The hardmen are cheering away like the Celtic end at Ibrox during an Old Firm 'clash' with Rangers. And I only support Kilmarnock!

The game's over now. Goodbye cruel school . . .

78

Suddenly, the door swings open as flying bodies scramble back to desks and silence spreads through the room.

'Ya'd better do what the lassie says,' a familiar deep voice calls out from behind me. 'Leave him alone *noo*.'

Spinning round with a huge grin on my face, I've never been so glad to see Rab Guthrie in my life-that-nearly-ended-there-in-a-pool-of-curry-sauce. I'm suddenly back to my usual cool dude self again!

'He's with me,' Rab says. 'So's the wee yin over there.' Rab winks at Sally then flexes his pecs for The *Big Fight* fans in the ringside seats.

'OK,' Slimey says. 'I'll let him off this time. But only because he's with you, Rab.'

Sure it's not because the hardmen are with Rab, Slimeball? And they well outnumber yer scrum!

Slimey drills his killer look through me. 'Just watch it, Burns. I've got your registration number now.'

'If there's any letting off to do –' Rab fires a rasper of a fart – 'I'll be doing it. Then ya can all watch oot.' He rips off another roaster. 'Register that, folks, that was number two. And three's on the way right noo . . .'

Everyone starts laughing. And me more than anybody. Rab's just saved the National Health Service two hundred quid's worth of emergency dental repair treatment here.

Slimey grins. 'How's it going anyway, Rab?'

'That's oor star striker there, y'know.' Rab crunches his fingers slowly, one at a time, as he nods over at me. 'He's in ma team.'

'Oh, aye, the cup final . . .' Slimey smiles, giving Rab the thumbs up sign. 'I'll be coming down to cheer you on, mate! You too, Burns.' He gives me the evil eye.

'Now that we've got that sorted,' Rab says, looking round the room. 'Whose turn is it tonight tae do ma homework fur me?'

I love it when Rab flexes his pecs.

12

'Thanks for sticking up for me in there, you two,' Sally says, grinning, when we get out of school and head down the road.

'Don't thank me,' I tell her. 'The heavy-weight champion of the school is right here.' I give Rab a soft jab in the side.

'Nae problem,' Rab says, ignoring me, nodding at Sally. 'I always look after my mates.' He pretends to throw a punch at Sal, then laughs. 'I heard that tongue-lashing ya were givin' Slimey Climie halfway doon the corridor, y'know. I like a girl with guts who can stand up for herself. Yur a wee tiger underneath that Liverpool strip.'

Sally's face goes as red as the footie top we can see through her school blouse. She looks like a little angel next to big bad Rab.

'That was some party piece in there, big man,' she says. 'Fartin' on command, eh? You'll have to teach me that wee trick.'

I grin at Rab as I hold in the laughing gas. Bless her. Doesn't she know yet that girls can't fart like us?

Rab chuckles. 'I took fartin' lessons from ma

big sister. Oor Tracy can fire 'em off like an Uzi sub-machine gun when she's had beans on toast. You'll pick it up nae problem, Sal pal.'

I give Sally a sideways glance. I didn't know girls had nuclear warhead capabilities. I thought they could only do silent farts? Well, I've never heard a girl guffing before. I thought they had some sort of in-built sound absorber like a car exhaust pipe – so they don't give babies brain damage when they're pregnant. Makes sense, doesn't it? When you think about it, I mean. Whoever would have guessed it, eh? Girls with secret DIY Jacuzzi bubble bath facilities just like the lads! See, I'm learning something new about girls every day now!

Rab wraps his hairy arms round Sally and me as we reach our street, and gives us both a bear hug goodbye. 'Gotta go, guys. Gotta chick to pick up at half six.'

'Who's the lucky lass tonight?' I ask him.

'You tell me,' he laughs. 'Not even I can keep up with ma hectic love life these days!'

I grin. 'Another hot date at the Late Cafe?'

'I'm double-booked, actually. Ya couldn't help a mate oot on a blind date, couldja?' He gives me the old nudge-nudge, wink-wink, phworrr-phworrr face. '*Very* un-ugly looking. We're talkin' Babe here with a capital B. She's got massively HUGE—'

'Sorry, Rab,' Sally says. 'He's got football training with me tonight in his back garden.'

We both look at Sally with mild surprise

82

turning to shock, pretending we never heard that alternative little suggestion of hers there.

'Have ya forgotten the cup final next week?' she says.

'Oh, aye,' Rab says, as if he's suddenly just remembered the big day.

I'd almost forgotten about it myself. Babe with a capital B, eh? Same A-class as Melanie A, eh? Massively HUGE . . . Well, I'm not even daring to think about it with wee Sally standing there. Let's just say W is for Woman – not Wonderbra.

Rab laughs. 'The only kind of work-out this goalkeeper needs is a night oot with the girls. All I have to do is stand there and watch Joey scoring the goals.' He pats Sally softy on the back. 'Make sure ya have oor star striker squat-jumping all over the stadium, darlin'.' Then he slaps me hard on the shoulder. 'Ya hotshot, yeh! After ya win us the cup, Braveheart, ya can score with any babe I set ya up with.'

'First,' Sally says, 'he has to *win* us the cup.'

We're outside my front gate.

'Don'tcha sometimes wish you had brothers or sisters?' I ask Sally.

'Sometimes,' she says, 'when I see my pals with their brothers and sisters. But then, some-times, when I do see them, I think: Thank God I *don't* have any brothers or sisters! I'm glad I'm an only child.'

'Me, too. It's better just to be friends like us.'

83

Sally sighs. 'Whadaya want now?'

'You know . . .'

'Am I supposed to guess?' She sounds amused. 'At least give me a clue to the subject.'

'*Snogging*. Ya promised to help me score with Melanie Anderson.'

'Somehow I thought it might be that.'

I laugh. 'Ya sure ya don't mind . . . about me and Mel dating, I mean? I'll have to cut back the football practice with you, y'know.'

'Let's get you a date first, huh? But first –' she shoves me against the gate – 'we have to work out how to cancel Silmey Climie from the equation.'

'The home team,' I say.

'The home team,' Sally says.

And as I drop the latch on the gate and it squeaks slowly open, Laddie runs barking across the grass to greet us.

13

'I hated . . . seeing you . . . in detention . . . with all those . . . hardmen,' I gasp, gazing up at Sally as I flop down on the grass, knackered.

'You're so sweet,' she says. '*Ten more press-ups.*'

Sally's really putting me through my paces in the stadium tonight. The game has gone on longer than usual as we get some extra practice in for the cup final, but now we can't see the ball any more, even in the fluorescent glow of the kitchen window floodlights. So Sally's got the old whip out for a quick fitness and stamina session, and wee Laddie's sitting on the touch-line – probably wondering what the score is with his madman master. He looks tired, too, just watching me!

'C'mon, Sal,' I call out. 'It'll soon be time for supper!'

'There's no slackers in my team, hotshot. Two . . . Three . . . Come on! . . . Four . . .'

'Yer a—'

'Five . . . Six . . . Move it, slacker!'

'Eight-nine-ten . . . Yer a wee slave driver, Taylor.' I stand up, then bend over, hands on my knees, breathing heavily. 'What I was trying to tellya,' I go on, glancing up at her, 'is that I take it personally when I see someone ribbing you like Slimey Climie was doing.'

'Really . . .?'

'Well, you're one of my best mates, Sal.'

'And . . .?'

'And my next door neighbour as well. I've got to look out for ya. It's like an unwritten law between us. I see it as my duty, almost.' I really do. I would do anything to help or protect Sally. I mean I would have . . . If Rab had given me the chance to kill Slimey before he jumped in to save me . . . I mean jumped in on my side.

'*Right*! Thirty sit-ups . . . *now*!'

'No way, *coach*.' I've had enough of her slave labour for one night. 'Ya think I'm yer boyfriend or something – giving orders like that?'

'If you didn't get detention for being so stupid, Braveheart, you'd be in there having yer tea.'

'You got detention as well,' I tell Sally. 'Let me remind *you*.'

'Whadaya think I am – one goal short of a hat-trick? I'm not in training for a cup final – I'm not that stupid. And besides – down Laddie, down boy . . .' She gives Laddie a big cuddle as he nuzzles his nose against her grass-stained goalie's top. 'We know why *I* got detention. *You*, a writer?'

'So you've heard about my infamous story, then?'

'Oh, everybody knows about *that*, Joey.' She pauses. 'How come ya never asked me to help ya write it?'

'*You*?'

'Eh, I've just joined the school newspaper as a cub reporter, I'll have ya know.' Sally folds her arms and taps a foot as if she's expecting some kind of answer or apology.

'Cub's the word, kid,' I tease her. 'My story was more adults-only, if y'know worra mean.'

Aww, she's getting huffy on me. Aww, what did I say now?

I go to give her a big brotherly hug, just to show I'm only joking, but she slips out from under my arms.

'Oh, I know what you mean all right, Joey Burns, with your adults-only *lads* humour. Morag McAdam told me all about yer saucy wee story. So when ya gonna show me a copy?'

Boy, when Sally wants to know something – she wants to know all right.

'I told ya, Cub. It was too adults-only for you. Anyway, old Wilma Rubber Fingers ripped it up.'

'Ya could have at least let me read it first. I could have toleja if yer female characters were believable.'

'Oh, they were believable all right.' The words 'big boobs' and 'long legs' flash through my mind, I don't know why. 'Written from a boy's point of view, of course.'

'All description and no characterisation, then.'

'Whadaya mean?'

'Think about it like an adult for once in yer sad lad's life.'

As we grab our kit up off the grass and I go to put the ball away in the kitchen cupboard, Sally says, 'Can I interview ya for the cup final, Joey?'

'For the *School Voice*?' I laugh.

'Go on, Joey, let me interview ya. Y'know you'll be the man of the match.'

I grin. 'Who have *you* interviewed before? Show me some of yer articles first.'

'You'll be the first.'

'Oh, no . . .'

'C'mon, hotshot, gimme a break. A cub reporter's gotta start somewhere, y'know.'

'Not with me ya won't.'

I watch Sally fill Laddie's water bowl then pour tea into two mugs from the pot my mum's left stewing for us on the cooker.

'Two sugars, please, waitress,' I say, all smiley-like.

Plunk, plunk . . . tinkle, tinkle . . . teaspoon thunks against the sink.

No pally *parlez* from Sally, though. Next she'll be pulling the big freeze treatment and totally ignoring me till I finally give in to her. I'm starting to thaw already at the sight of that steaming hot tea. Sally always manages to get her way with me in the end. I hate it when she has the hump about something. Girls!

'I don't know, Sal.'

'Go on . . .' She holds some biscuits teasingly at arm's length, then sighing, hands them over to me. 'If I interview ya, Melanie Anderson'll get to read the article first before it gets printed. It's her job as Features Editor . . . to be the bitch with a blue pen.'

'Oh, so Mel *is* on the paper,' I lie. 'I thought Mr Lovett did it.'

'She's practically the editor, y'know. After Mr Lovett, I mean. He's like the big editor-in-chief.'

'Hey . . .' I suddenly realise what she's just said. 'Less of the bitchy language.' Sally might be one of my best mates but she's not bad-mouthing my girlfriend-by-the-time-we've-won-the-cup like that. 'If Melanie Anderson's holding a blue pen over your work, Cub, then she's probably got good reason.'

'C'mon, Joey. Think about it. She'll be able to read *all* about you. All about Joey Burns . . .'

'Mmmmn.' I'm very interested now. If I let Sally interview me they might even put a picture of me in the paper and then Mel baby really will get to know me. She might even cut the pin-up out and stick it on the headboard on her bed; secretly fancying me, too.

'Hmmmn, there's just one little detail you've over-looked in your writer's research.'

'And what's that?' Sally asks, sceptically.

'Er, Slimey Climie . . .'

She smiles. 'Not a problem. The rugby team

89

got knocked out in the quarter-finals of the school cup, yeah? He's history, pal. You're the man of the match now.'

'Ya really think so?'

'Dunno.' Sally shrugs. 'You tell me. Yer gonna have to convince me yerself . . . when I interview ya for the *School Voice.*'

'What questions ya gonna ask anyway?' There's no harm in knowing what Melanie will read about me if I go on the record about still being available for the right girl in my life.

'Y'know, Joey . . . when did you first realise you had the potential to succeed in soccer, what are your aspirations for furthering your education at university . . . the usual school bull.'

'Oh, I don't know. Those kind of interviews always make you look as if you fancy yourself.'

Take the one Slimey Climie gave at the start of the rugger season, for example. What a puke! Lucky the free gift in that issue was a rugby-shaped sick bag . . .

'I'll be writing it, remember,' Sally says. 'I might even letcha read it first.'

I sigh. 'OK, I'm prepared to give you a break. I'll do the interview! I'll do it! Now no further comment . . .'

'So we've got a deal, then?'

As I offer up the old sacrificial hand, Sally drops to her knees and shakes one of Laddie's paws. 'It's a done deal, partner. Witnessed in the presence of Laddie Taylor Burns.'

'Now that you've got a half share in our dog, it's your turn to take him for a walk.'

We're saying g'night to each other at the garden gate. Only Sally's hanging back a little bit as if she doesn't want to go into her own house just yet. Then, all of sudden, when I'm wondering what Sally wants to say, she says, 'D'you think I'm nice looking, Joey?'

I look at Sally looking at me.

'You're probably the nicest girl I know.'

'I said *looking* – not personality. Have I got what it takes to get guys going?'

I really look at Sally now. 'What's come over *you* all of a sudden?'

She sighs. 'D'you think I'm too boyish-looking – for a girl, I mean?'

So that's what's on her mind? Slimey Climie was well out of order with his nasty wind-up patter.

'Forget what Slimeball said,' I tell her. 'It's just a phase you're going through. Maybe you should just dress – I don't know – more like a girl.' Then I quickly add, 'Instead of tracksuit and trainers all the time, I mean.'

'Oh aye, wise guy, I can just see myself tottering at the edge of the penalty box in towering wedge shoes and a satin slip dress. Get real, ya *moron*! Ya sound just like my maw sometimes.'

Ah, good old Sally's back in goals. She's one of the lads again now. I'm glad she's snapped out of that funny little mood she was in. I've never seen her acting like this before. I could kill Slimey Climie. I mean I would have . . . if Rab hadn't jumped in!

14

The rain falls lightly on us as we get into our football kit up North Beach. Since we all wanted the extra Sunday morning practice for the cup final – just three days away now – we can't really complain about the bad weather and the waterlogged pitch. Only, we'd rather get on with the game than stand around shivering in our shorts and T-shirts while we help the coach kick seaweed off the sand.

'Did you bring towels like I asked you to?' Mr Lovett nods across at the kitbags piled up on the grass at the edge of the beach.

'Aye, sir,' we answer, not knowing why.

We all watch the coach, waiting, as the whispering surf pounds the shore.

'Oh, naw, sur,' Rab says. 'I forgot ma suntan lotion.'

Lovett grins. 'We're not going for a swim, lads. We're going to play a little Brazilian football; like they do on the beach in Rio de Janeiro.'

We all look at each other.

'Barefoot on the sand,' the coach says. He means the cold, wet sand sticking to our

93

trainers. 'But only for a couple of minutes. The water's way too cold. I don't want any of you going down with the kind of flu Joey's just had; not the week of the final.'

I'm glad he's noticed – 'cause I notice he's not taking his trainers off to join us. I remember my dad and I playing without shoes on the beach, when I was a nipper and he could still run. He said it's good for getting a natural feel for the ball and that's why the Brazilian players have such brilliant football skills. But there's one big difference between Ardrossan and Rio: those palm tree goal posts they have on Brazilian beaches would never grow up here – even in summer. Now I know why old Lovett doesn't teach geography. And this is supposed to be the warm-up? My feet are frozen as we run through the shallow water like a bunch of raw Navy Seals recruits. More male bonding, sir, eh? I'm glad we're not playing with the ball yet, 'cause I don't fancy getting splashed as well. The water's fr-r-r-r-eezing!

'That's enough, lads,' Lovett says finally. He signals us to stop.

I quietly ask, 'Are we finished bonding yet, sir?'

'Ya not supposed to do this in summer, sir?' wee Davie Wilson says, skinny and anaemic looking, shivering away like a waif supermodel in a photographer's draughty studio. 'When it's warm and sunny?'

Maybe old Lovett doesn't know. Maybe he'll

get the message now that we're all freezing our butts off. Brrr!

'You're right, lads.' He waves us out of the water. 'But I won't be here then to show you.'

'Ya leaving, sir?' I say, not understanding.

Rab speaks first. 'Naw, we're leavin' . . . *thicko.*'

'Oh, aye . . . school's out for summer,' I say, hoping it's going to be for good this year.

Ben Robinson sourly smiles. 'Speak for yourself, Burnsie. I'm staying on for sixth year.'

'Me, too,' Ronnie Cowan says, not looking at us.

A sudden thought comes to me. 'We could always start up one of those amateur league sides in our spare time – like the pub teams that play on Sundays.'

'Blindin' idea,' Rab laughs. 'We could play against all the pub teams – then get slaughtered with them after the game.'

'Only one problem, Joey,' Ben says with a smirk on his face. 'You'd be useless in a pub team. Ya don't even drink shandy.'

'Zip it, spamhead,' Rab tells him.

Ben glares back. 'What's beefin' you, ya big bloater?'

'Sod off,' Rab snaps. 'Ya baldy big—'

'Language, lads,' Lovett says. 'C'mon now, it's too cold to stand around in your bare feet. Get your socks and trainers on and we'll start the game.'

I'm glad Lovett jumped in there 'cause I

don't need a reminder about my drink problem; not in front of the others. Ben probably never realised what he was saying; about my dad, I mean. Even so, Ben's been getting a bit cocky for my liking these days. I know Rab wasn't just sticking up for me. Things have become tense between the two of them lately, and I don't know why. They used to be such good mates.

We move over to the flat patch of grass near the beach and dump our kitbags down for goalposts. Old Lovett's a top bloke all the same, I'm thinking as I help him carry the balls from the school gym. He's got them packed inside his nifty two-seater white MG sports car parked at the side of the road. I'm going to get a babemobile like that when I turn professional. Just room for me and Mel baby and no backseat Maw drivers.

'Ya live near here, sir?' I ask him as he locks the car door.

'No, I've got a small pad over by Saltcoats shorefront. Near the Bay Hotel.'

'Oh, right . . .' It's all posh houses and flats over that way. 'Ya like it up here, then?'

'Everyone's been really friendly. You notice the change coming from a big city like London. Glasgow's pretty much the same.'

'Too crowded, sir.'

'Yeah, people keep to themselves, I suppose. All with their own little lives. You could live in the same flat there for years and not know anyone who stays in the same building.'

'How come you're going to college in Glasgow?'

'My mother's side of the family are Scottish.'

'Really?'

'We've still got a lot of relatives up here. It seemed like a good opportunity to find out more about my heritage and get a teaching degree at the same time.'

'Ya made any friends yet, sir?'

'Not really. I seem to be working all the time.' He smiles at the other lads warming up on the pitch. 'Or taking homework away with me to correct in the evening.'

It's his day off today, as well. With the sun starting to come out now, he could be away anywhere for the day instead of being stuck here with us football-mad lads.

'Seen much of Scotland since you've been here, sir?'

'I travelled around a bit before college started, at the end of last summer. I went up to Loch Lomond, Loch Ness, took the ferry over to Skye. The water was way too choppy, though. Worse than it is out there . . .' He gestures toward the whitecaps breaking against the harbour wall in the far distance. 'I haven't really had much chance for sightseeing since I got the job.'

'It'll soon be the summer holidays. Students get six weeks off like us, don'tcha?'

'Yeah, there's that to look forward to . . .' His sentence sort of trails off as the team stud joins us, joking as usual.

'What aboot snog partners, sur? Met any Scottish wuman yet?'

'Guthrie,' Lovett says, turning red. 'Is that all you can think about?'

I feel a bit awkward, so I hand Rab a ball, quickly.

'That's right,' Lovett tells him, 'help Joey. Make yourself useful now.'

'I thought we were supposed tae be team *mates*,' Rab says, a little uncertainly.

'So let's just try and keep it that way, Guthrie.'

A sudden reminder that although he's dead easy going, he's still our teacher. Rab's right, though. No matter how much you think you're talking openly to teachers, they never really tell you anything about their personal life. I suppose it's like mixing business with pleasure. All that keep it in the classroom crap, don't get too involved with pupils. I still think he's a top bloke all the same, even though I don't really know him at all.

Oh, but he's a crafty footballer, though. All a teacher has to do really is coach us and then referee when the game gets going and maybe discipline us a bit if we get carried away and start tearing into each other like Ben and Rab when they lost the rag with each other earlier. But old Lovett always manages to blag his way into the game and now he's on the ball and charging past me. I try to run level with him but I've never realised how fast he is. He's got good ball control as well, always shielding it with his body to make tackling difficult. But then he makes the mistake of staying on the wing too long instead of cutting into the midfield, which is what I would have done. So I slide right in there and knock the ball out from under his feet as we both go tumbling over on our backs on the wet slippery grass.

'Nice one, Joey,' Lovett laughs as the rest of the team crowd round us and help us to our feet.

I like it when someone can take a tackle without getting all stroppy; especially when it's a clean, fair tackle. I told you, he's a top bloke for a Chelsea and an England supporter.

'Been to any football matches yet?' big Ronnie Cowan asks the coach as we carry the balls over to his car at the end of the practice session. Our team captain's a huge Rangers supporter, by the way. Bet he's trying to find out which Scottish team Teach supports. It's weird how everybody wants to know what old Lovett likes; shows the effect he's had on all of us, and not just me.

'Only on television,' he says, laughing. 'I just don't have the time to go to matches now.'

'Ya could always come to a Killie game on the supporters' bus. With me and Rab,' I say.

Rab and I look up in stunned disbelief as a dozen bodies pile on top of us.

After we leave the others, Rab and I head home. Rab's house is at the bottom end of Strathclyde Avenue, but he carries on walking with me along Eglinton Road, and then we turn right at the High Tide pub and go over the old railway bridge down into my street.

'I thought ya had yer Sunday roast to go to?' I say, surprised. 'It's sacrilege to miss it in your house.'

'Don't worry aboot me, boy. I'm no' hungry.'

Rab's dad works in the slaughterhouse, by the way. So does Rab's big brother, Mick. Rab will probably be punching the old shift work clock-card with them when he clocks out of school in the summer. The Guthries love meat. I mean, they can't get enough of it.

I grin. 'My maw'll probably be round my gran's house.'

'Good, ya can break open the Kit-Kats with the coffee. I'm dyin' fur some choccers.'

'I thought ya weren't hungry?'

Rab says nothing. Then he says, 'Ya no' want me round or something?'

'Don't be soft. Y'know I hate being alone after football training.'

'I know what ya mean, mate. It leaves me on a high as well.' Rab throws a soft jab to the shoulder, smiling. 'He's a fly guy all the same, old Lovett.'

'Whatja mean?'

'Ya heard me askin' him up the beach if he was snoggin' anybody.'

'Is he?'

'Some blonde bird, apparently. So he's obviously tryin' tae keep it a secret from the boys.'

'*Howja know*?' I want to know.

'Oor Mick saw him in his sports car with a *very* snoggable babe.'

'Ya know who it was?'

'Nah, Mick only got a glimpse of her as the car sped past.'

'How did Mick know it was Lovett?'

'Who else drives a white MG with a big GB sticker on the back bumper.'

'I wish he'd seen her, Rab. I'd love to know who he's snogging.'

'Unless, of course, the bird was his sister.'

'Has Lovett got a sister?'

'Dunno.'

'We know nothing about him, do we?'

'Only that he's a fast worker, Joey boy. Lovett with a babe, eh?'

I'm thinking that very soon I'll be in the same situation as *sir*. A dream job, when I sign with Ardrossan Rovers. A dream machine, when I pass my driving test. A dream babe, when I pull Melanie Anderson. I've got it all to look forward to . . .

'We're playing Rangers in the last league match of the season; the end of May. Why don'tcha come with us, sir?'

'It's very nice of you to ask. But—'

We hear the familiar laddish laughter and then Rab's up beside us, saying, 'We'll no' tell them yur a student teacher, sur. Honest.'

That's what he is, though. And he can't be seen to be socialising with pupils outside school hours.

Lovett grins. 'I really wonder what goes on in your head sometimes, Guthrie.'

'So do all the other teachers,' Ben calls out. 'That's why they're kickin' him out this year.'

I can see Rab's fingers clenching into fists and so can Mr Lovett.

'Now, lads,' the coach tells the class, suddenly a teacher again. 'The game's still another month away. Let's just wait and see, shall we?'

I'm not waiting. 'We're gonna scud ya, Cowan.'

'Gimme a break, Burnsie. When have Killie ever beat the Gers?'

'Right noo,' Rab yells. 'Get him, Joey.'

We both jump on big Ronnie and hold him down as he squeals for help.

'Who's gonna win?' Rab shouts, twisting his knuckles in at the back of Ronnie's neck.

'Bog off!' Ronnie screams. 'Ya big bloater!'

'Ya give in,' I say, laughing away.

'Get them, lads,' Mr Lovett shouts.

15

Monday night I nip next door to Sally's house, but she doesn't sound as happy to see me as she was on the blower five minutes ago when she asked me over.

'Not Melanie Anderson again,' Sally says, closing the bedroom door behind her. 'You said it was important.'

'And you said you'd help me get off with her. Those were the exact words you used.' I give her my best *best mate* smile. 'C'mon, Sal, I need some expert girlie help here . . . I'm a desperate man.'

'And the words you used were: *School Voice. Exclusive. Promise.*'

I pull another kind of face. 'Oh, I don't know . . .'

'Remember, Joey. Melanie Anderson'll read all about ya; the glowing report I'll give ya. This is yer big chance to make an impression on her without even standing in front of her and stuttering.'

'Are you sure she'll read it?'

'The whole school's going to read it!'

'Aye, and that's *why* I don't want to do it.'

'If you can't help me, then I can't help you.'

'Oh . . . whadaya wanna know, anyway?'

'Not now.'

'*What?*'

'My friend Morag's due round any minute.'

The doorbell rings.

'That's her.'

'I'd better beat it, then.'

'Unless ya fancy a girlie night in. Hey, maybe Morag can come up with some suggestions for yer sad lad's love life, too.'

'I'm outta here!'

And then I'm up off the bed and at the door.

'That's right, soft lad, take a hike. I'll see ya tomorrow night.'

I swing round.

'It's the night before the cup final.'

'All the better to get a pre-match buzz going. Unless, of course, ya don't really need those coaching lessons after all . . .'

Now she's waving me away.

'Go on, Morag's waiting. Let her in when you leave.'

'Aye, and bye-bye to you, too.'

I dive down the stairs as the doorbell rings again. I let Sally's pal in, and as I squeeze past her in the hall to get out, the big lanky beanpole brushes against me, giggling, giving me a quick whiff of her old granny's perfume.

Maybe Morag can come up with some suggestions?

Gimme a break, darlin'!

As I go to close the front door behind me, I notice Sal's gangly gal pal is still standing there; gazing at me with Bambi eyes, if you must know.

'Hello, Joey,' she says shyly, fidgeting with this polybag in her hands, getting all gushy and giggly again with that look on her freckly face that I know only to well. That look that says: so this is him; this is what the love god looks like up close and personal. She's actually quite un-ugly, I have to admit; for a mousy-haired bean-pole pal of Sal's, I mean. Still too immature for a man of the world like me, of course. I'll have to remember to keep my eye on her, though; keep her on the old substitute bench for a year or two until she grows up and fills out in the bod a bit and gets the blonde streaks in her wig and that before I let her join my fan club. Hey, hold back the teen idol adulation, *purlease*! It even looks as if the chick's dying to get some practice in for me already; judging by that hair dye I can see through the flimsy polybag. Morag's her name, is it? Aye, I must remember that.

'Go right on up, *Morag*. Sally's waiting for ya.'

I give her a quick flash of my killer smile. Then, without even waiting to see her swoon at my feet, I run and jump over the fence into my garden with only one hand on the post, nearly breaking my crazy hotshot neck.

16

'A couple of the lads are with me. Jay and Ben,' Rab's telling me. 'We're at the phone box in Glasgow Street, the foot of Cannon Hill. Ya comin' doon, boy?'

'Ten minutes, mate. I'm on the way.'

'We'll be up at the castle waitin' fur ya.'

I slam the phone down, pick up my keys, grab my jacket, and I'm outta here! It's not even an hour yet since Sally kicked me out; only about seven-ish now. I mean, I'm not that desperate for company, don't get me wrong. I'm not *that* bored. I never get bored. I can stand my own company, no problem. Lucky Morag came round to Sal's house after all. Aye, and they can shove their girlie night in. I'm going on a lads night out!

Bombing out of the house, I bump into Sally and Morag, who are also on the way out, I can see. All babed-up in girlie gear and standing at the gate!

'Want anything from the ice-cream van, Joey?' Morag shouts as she runs across the road and gets in the queue outside the Mr Freeze van that's just pulled up at the kerb in a blare of music and a cloud of exhaust fumes.

I tell her no and grin at Sal, who's – *what's this*! – wearing a dress!

'Hi again,' Sally says smiling, as she slips her coat on against the nippy chill in the air.

Before I can ask her if it's the same trendy little black number that that supermodel wears on the telly ad, Morag calls out, 'Want some chuggy, Sal?'

'Yes, please,' Sally calls back.

'Gettin' the Extra spearmint gum in now that yer snoggin' boys, eh?'

'Aye, we're goin' on the pull tonight, pal.'

'Where ya off to anyway?' I ask, curious. 'I thought ya were havin' a girlie night in?'

'We're goin' clubbing – is it not obvious.'

'Another under-fourteen disco down the youth club, eh?'

'I'm *fifteen*, Joey Burns!' Sally looks me straight in the eyes. 'It was my birthday two weeks ago – and you forgot it again!'

How was I supposed to know that she's fifteen? Come to think of it, you know, it is kinda obvious. Now that I know. Now that I'm looking at her, like. Wearing a bra, eh? I'm wondering if it really *is* the old wonderbra Sally's got on? I mean I've never noticed anything there before. Not that I've been looking, mind. But now that I think about it, I kind of, you know, can't keep my eyes away from her in

107

that, you know, *general direction*. Sally with a bra, eh?

I suddenly notice her staring at me. She's probably waiting for some kind of compliment about her dress. Girls *always* want you to tell them how gorgeous they look when they're decked out in new togs.

'Wearing the old away strip,' I say, jokingly.

'I got it in Glasgow. Ya like it?'

'Dunno . . .' I'm being completely honest with her here. I mean how am I supposed to know about girlie gear? I'm only a lad. A dress is just a dress to me. 'It looked all right on that supermodel, I suppose.'

'Aye, well, the next dress I'll be wearing in public, pal, will be ma wedding dress.' She turns to walk away.

What's wrong with *her* tonight?

'And there's me thinking you'd be walking up the aisle in yer Liverpool strip,' I say for a laugh, letting her know that I think she looks really nice in her new girlie gear away kit. 'With the maids of honour all dressed up as ball boys, huh?'

'Enjoy the show, Joey, when you've got the chance.'

'Naw, you look really fit, Sal. Straight up.'

But she starts walking away again.

'Willya be wearing a wonderbra on yer wedding day as well?' I whisper after her, all innocent-looking, all straight-faced, like, as she spins round. Got her now! Look at the beamer!

Beet-*root*! I knew it was the old cotton-wool-stuffed-up-yer-jumper trick. You can't fool me with falsies. I mean I should know – I practically *invented* the concept. And I don't mean I was trying on my mum's big green bra when she was down the chippie, either. No, I'm talking about the *wonderballs* I used to wear when I shoved a scrunched-up sock down my trunks at Auchenharvie Swimming Pool. I mean, I don't do it any more. I haven't done it for ages now. I don't even go to the pool any more.

Sally leans closer, lowering her voice. 'Get real, Joey. D'ya think my maw would let me wear a wonderbra – never mind ma dad?'

Get real indeed, eh? Sally with boobs? I can't believe it, to be honest. I'm beginning to look at old Sally the goalkeeper in another way now. That figure-hugging dress really brings out the womanly shape-to-be in her. Just goes to show what tracksuits and baggy football strips do for a girls budding sex appeal. Soon Sally will be going on the pull . . . and snogging boys, too!

Sally smiles. 'Notice anything else different about me?'

How do I know? She's got make-up on her mug and everything tonight!

'Gimme a couple of minutes and I'll tell ya.'

'Oh, don't bother . . .'

'It's just an all-round difference,' I tell her, though I can't exactly put my finger on it just yet and be specific. Sally seems satisfied with that. For the moment.

'Ya really think so?'

'Yer a regular substitute supermodel.'

'So, I'm gorgeous now? You're calling me a babe, eh?'

'One dress doesn't make you Supermodel Sal. Not when you've got footballer's legs and that shin injury there to prove it.'

Sally lowers her gaze to the graze that's almost gone now, her face matching the colour of the fading mark on her leg.

'I was only joking, Joey.'

Oh, I know it was a terrible thing to say. I don't know why I said it 'cause it wasn't even funny. I didn't mean it to come out that way. Sally's got really nice legs, if you must know. They're not sparrow legs and they're not tree trunks either. They're just normal nice legs. I didn't mean to upset her. Tonight of all nights, when she's going out with her mate.

'Look, Sal, you look really *lovely* and that . . .' I nod over at Morag who's crossing the street. Aye, and coming straight at us with a big grin on her face. Now I've really got to go . . .

'I'll get ya down the road a bit,' I tell the girls. Well, they're going my way anyway. I have to go by the crummy youth club to get to Castle Hill. Aye, and they'd better not hold me back with their high heels and girlie gossip either. The lads are waiting on me!

It feels kind of weird walking with Sally all

grown-up looking in her girlie gear; the click of high heels on the hard concrete pavement; the wild mane of hair blowing around her shoulders in the cool night breeze. The funny thing is, though, I sort of like it. I really do. I'm quite glad of the company after all.

'I know what's different about ya,' I say as it suddenly clicks. 'You've done something with yer wig, haven't ya?' I give her gal pal a nod. 'Morag's been giving you the old DIY make-over, hasn't she?'

'Just a rinse,' Morag says.

Sally flicks reddish highlights away from the smile on her face. 'Ya like it?'

'Took ages for me to spot it in the dark,' I tell them. 'I thought it was just the orange glow from the streetlights. One of those wash-out jobs? The old *hint of a tint*, eh?'

'Aye,' Sally says.

'Thought so. Ya can see it a mile away once you know. Better being safe than sorry, eh? Aye, those permanent ones are pure murder to get out.' I start grinning. 'Remember when Rab Guthrie sprayed blue and white dye on his barnet during the last World Cup? Oh, it was priceless, Sal. I couldn't stop killing myself!'

'I know what you mean, *butthead*.' Sally wallops me one in the stomach, then turns on her high heels and stomps away. 'I could kill you, too!'

'*What was that for?*' I stare at her back,

doubling over as I hold my stomach. What have I done now?

Without turning round, Sally shouts out, 'You're so immature sometimes, *butthead*!'

'I'm sorry, Sally.' I really am. Even though I don't know what I've said. 'Hey, and what's the unflattering nickname for?'

I chase after Sally and, as I catch up with her, I say, 'Hey, I've said I was sorry,' even though I'm not too sure what for.

'You will be one day,' she says, 'but I'll forgive you for now.'

I still don't know what she's on about.

Morag's grinning at us, and then they both start giggling.

I quickly look away, saying, 'The lads are waiting. Have a nice night now, girls. I've gotta run . . .'

17

Some people call it Cannon Hill, others call it
Castle Hill. It's all the same to me, really. All
it is are these crumbly old ruins on top of this
big grass hill in Ardrossan. From where we're
sitting on the castle wall, we've got a brilliant
view below us of the black empty waters of the
Firth of Clyde, glittering in the South Beach
promenade lights. It's dead dark and spooky up
here at night, even with the fire Rab Guthrie's
got going with grass and twigs supposedly to
keep us warm. It's dead windy too, no shelter,
that's why it's so cold. I'm freezing my butt
off. We all are. Jason, Ben, Rab and me. The
Fantastic Four we call ourselves, when we're
chilling out.

Aaaahhh . . . The castle central heating is
blazing away now. We found some broken
branches lying over in the trees and tossed them
on the old camp fire. Beautiful! Let's just hope
the Neighbourhood Watch don't spot the
flames and call the cops, eh? Aye, we're a team
tonight, all right. I'm glad Rab and Ben have
managed to patch up their differences after
flying off the rails with each other at football

training yesterday. I'm not saying that they plan to run round the male bonding camp-fire later on in thermal Iron John pants. They've not bonded that close yet – and we're not bonding that close *ever*.

Ben's an all right bloke, really, just like Rab and Jason. He's a bit snobby, though. Well, his dad is. His dad's a top local lawyer. Smart suit and smug looking, if you know what I mean. With the kind of gifted, natural, friendly charisma that can send a deathly hush through a room whenever he walks in. Ben boy's the same – except he's still got hair. Sandy and receding already on his big bone dome. Ben's old man has been courting him with the offer of a full partnership in the family law firm when he graduates from college. That's what Ben's been telling us as we talk about leaving school in the summer.

'Still set on the Marines?' I ask Jason when Ben finishes.

Rab says, 'Thought ya were driving tanks with the artillery, Jay?'

Jason's smile shifts down a gear. 'I've been accepted for the Marines noo. I join up in August. The Commando Training Centre in Exmouth, Devon. Oh, I just have tae get away . . .' his voice cracks. 'I've had enough, man. It's doin' ma heed in at home.'

Oh, Jay. I want to say that I know what he's going through. That I've been through this kind of domestic bliss myself. But I know I'll sound too soft in front of the others. And the last thing I want to do is dredge up *my* happy family history again. Everybody knows it all anyway. I knew Jason was only signing up to get away from home. A Royal Marine Commando? I mean *come on*. He's practically a midget. A nice midget, all the same. Solid built, but small. Dead small. Action Man small.

You should see Jay on the pitch. He's a brilliant wee defender. A real pocket-size battleship of a bloke. Just wait till the army barber lops off his ponytail and gives him a skinhead. We'll not even recognise him when he comes home on leave every six months. They still call basic training square-bashing in the army, you know. Jason the pacifist, retreating from one war and invading another. His parents are like mine were: heading for a divorce ten years too late. At least I don't have to live through that battle-zone any more. I feel sorry for Jason. So does Rab.

'They've only got scrumpy doon in Devon,' Rab tells him. 'At least it's better than London, though. Oor Mick told me they don't even have any heavy doon there. It's called bitter. Aye, and I'd be bitter tae if I had to pay their prices.'

Jason grins. 'Ya'd better start savin' yer dosh then, Rab. The first round'll be on you when ya come down to visit me.'

'We'll no' be visitin' ya. We'll probably never see ya again, ya daft moron.'

'Whadaya mean, Rab?' I ask him.

'Look at Mick's mate, Tam Collins. He joined the Scots Guards and they packed him straight off to Germany. He's got an army hoose over there noo. Married to some German Helga wuman – way big boobs, tae!' Rab hollers.

A wave of laughter breaks out, and then Jason says, smiling, 'We can always have a team reunion in twenty years' time, lads.'

Rab chortles, 'When we're all fat and forty, ya mean.'

'You're already fat – ya big bloater,' Ben says, prodding Rab's wobbly gut with a piece of wood he then throws on the fire.

'That's muscle, mate,' Rab says, defensively. Well, he is the goalie, after all.

I quickly say, 'Lookin' forward to Wednesday night, lads?'

Jason returns my smile. 'I never ever thought I'd play at Rover Park. A real football ground, eh? That'll be your new pitch soon, Joey.'

'They haven't signed me yet,' I say, hoping they will. It's all I can think about now. My heart goes out to Jay again. I never want to be forced into doing something out of desperation like him, just to get away from home. I mean my maw doesn't bug me *that* much. I'd still want to live in Ardrossan.

'You should see some of the fall-back options my maw's been coming up with lately,' I tell the lads. 'Bank clerk, builder, electrician, plumber. She's about as original and inspiring as our

116

careers officer at school when she gets going. Football's not just a hobby to me, y'know.'

'Aye, I know what ya mean, mate.' Rab hesitates. 'I've got a wee interest myself that I practise in ma spare-time, tae; something that gives me more pleasure than fishing, stamp-collecting, playing golf, breakin' into shops and hooses. Ma hobby is—'

'Oh, give it a rest, Rab . . .' Ben pulls a face. 'We're tired of listening to yer stud talk, ya big blag.'

'I wasn't goin' tae – oh, forget I opened ma gob,' Rab says, getting all huffy on us now.

There's a silence, so I rustle up the fire a bit with a spare branch.

Ben turns to Jay and says, 'You're the lucky yin, y'know. At least you're gettin' away from home.'

'Aye, and I wish I was goin' with ya,' Rab says. 'Ya jammy wee bugger, yeh!'

Jay says, 'Well, yer all welcome to kip in ma flat any time ya want. Any time ya fancy a lads' holiday doon in Devon.'

'Yur no' gonna have a flat,' Rab tells him. 'They still make ya share barrack rooms with five other sweaty blokes. Ya only get an army hoose when yur stationed overseas with a wife. And y'know what happens then, mate.'

I grin. 'The kids take up the spare bedrooms so you have to kip on the sofa.'

'Aye, that as well,' Rab says. 'It's the wives, innit? They cut off all yur mates so you've got

117

none left apart from the ones they approve of –
the boring hen-pecked husbands of *their* mates.'

'Naw, that'll no happen to me,' Jason says.

'Same here,' Ben says.

'Me, too,' I say.

Rab says, 'You lot might have all the Standard Grades, but I'm tellin' ya, I'm more
prepared for the real world oot there than you'll
ever be.'

Ben laughs. 'What career ya planning to
follow anyway, Rab? Y'know they'll be kickin'
ya out of school after last year's performance.'

'I know ma art and metalwork Standards
won't get me far.' Rab grimly smiles. 'I'm not
even bothering to re-sit the subjects I failed
the first time – never mind taking the art and
metalwork Highers.'

Ben laughs again. 'Ya don't need qualifications to work in the slaughterhouse. The
name Guthrie is enough to get ya through the
cattle gate.'

'Watch it,' Rab warns. 'We don't all have a
cushy lawyer's job tae go tae in company cars.'

'Well yer not exactly office material, are ya,
mate?'

'I told ya, Ben boy.' Rab's gaze never leaves
his.

'We were all surprised when ya stayed on for
fifth year,' Jason says after a pause, saying what
we've all wanted to ask Rab for some time. 'We
thought you'd be straight in the slaughterhouse
with Mick and yer faither.'

'So what ya gonna do, Rab?' Ben asks.

'Sign on the dole?' Jay says.

'I'll tellya what big bad Rab Guthrie's gonna be when he leaves school.' Rab gets to his feet, grinning. 'Worse than I am noo! I'm no' the school stud for nowt, y'know!' Then he slips on the damp grass, still grinning away.

'Rab,' I say, taking him by the elbow to steady him. 'Watch ya don't go sliding down that hill in the dark.'

'On his big fat arse,' Ben laughs.

Rab pushes away from me. 'Oh, I've had enough of that baldy spamhead . . . Sod this, I'm goin' haim.'

'C'mon, Rab. Lighten up,' I say, still holding him by the arm.

Ben sniggers. 'You'll be late for the night-shift at the slaughterhouse, Rab, if ya don't hurry.'

'Ya baldy big—' Rab lunges at him.

Ben ducks Rab's punch, his fists at the ready. 'Ya wanna fight, ya big bloater?'

'Come into ma heed!' Rab takes another swing at Ben, who steps quickly out the way.

'Ya spamhead, yeh!'

'C'mon, lads. Stop it,' I say as Jason and I try to keep them from tearing into each other. 'We've got the cup final the day after tomorrow, for godsakes! We're supposed to be a team. Save the fighting talk for the Woodside lot!'

'Save it yurself, Joey,' Rab says. 'I'm outta

here.' And then he stomps away along the dark path into the houses at the bottom of the hill.

Ben glares at him as Jason raises his eyebrows at me.

'I'd better go after him,' I tell them. 'See you both at school tomorrow.'

I run after Rab and catch up with him in the lighted main street. We walk together, neither of us saying anything. Glancing over at Rab, I realise he's not as mad as I first thought.

I stare at him. 'What's wrong with you tonight – tearing into Ben like that? Why d'ya let him rile you so easily?'

'He's a right stuck-up jerk sometimes. We should kick him oot of the team and send him tae play with Slimey Climie's rugby scrum. He's more like them than us.'

'What's wrong?' I ask again.

'Nothin', mate.'

'That's right, Rab, I'm yer mate.'

He draws in a long, slow breath, then says, 'Ya all think I'm a waster, don't yeh? Ya think I can't get anythin' better than the slaughter-hoose?'

'I never said anything.'

'Naw, but ya were thinkin' it.' He looks directly at me. 'Weren't ya?'

'What *are* ya gonna do, then? Y'know they'll not let ya stay on another year at school.'

Rab goes silent on me again.

I shake my head. 'I mean who stays on at

school anyway – and then dogs half the classes on a regular basis.'

'Ya think I wanna stay on? I would have left already if it wasn't fur—'

'For what, Rab?'

'I dunno. I'll worry aboot it later.'

'Ya can't keep putting it off. There's only a few weeks left now till the end of term.'

He raises his voice. '*Ya think I don't know that?*'

I smile at him. 'We'll soon be free men, Rab! We've got our whole lives ahead of us. We can do whatever we want. Be anything we want. *Anything*, mate.'

'Ya really believe it, don'tcha?'

'*Don't you?*' I look at him, unbelieving.

'Yur such a dreamer, Joey boy.'

And then I think about my future job prospects if the Rovers don't sign me.

'Yer right, Rab.' I throw my arm round his shoulders as we head home in the dark. 'Dream on . . .'

We both break out with laughter.

Me and my best mate!

18

I'm sitting on top of Sally's bed the following night, watching her fiddling with this new fangled Dictaphone her dad's given her, to help 'encourage' her interest in journalism, no doubt. Sally's got it propped up on the bedside table, next to the open reporter's notebook filled with a million scribbled questions; all for me, by the looks of it. And I thought it was only going to be a quick five-minute interview.

I stifle a yawn, timing it with another quick glance at my watch as I slowly take my hand away from my mouth. Ten past seven already. Oh well – match of the day, eh? Time to blow the whistle.

'C'mon, Lois Lane. I haven't got all night, y'know. I need to get an early kip for the cup final tomorrow.'

'Nearly got it. Naw, that's not it.'

'Er . . . have ya tried pressing the play button yet?'

'I'll be pressing your PAIN button in a minute if ya don't pause it, pal.'

Girls!

I start yawning again – only this time I'm not

even looking at my watch. Sleepily, I sink back in the pile of soft toys that practically covers Sally's pit. Imagine trying to conk out with that technicolor dreamcoat lying on top of you like a ton of bricks. They wouldn't last five minutes in my bedroom. Laddie would eat them alive.

'Can yer detective dad nick me a tape recorder from the nick as well?'

'Whatja think this is, pal! A free Christmas prezzie from the gift catalogue they keep down the cop shop.'

'Does your *dad* know you talk like this? You'd better watch out he doesn't arrest you.' He probably would as well. 'Ya sure the room's not bugged?' It probably is as well. I'll bet Serious Sarge has got his big hairy ear up against the door right now.

'Hey, whose detective dad is it anyway? I can slag him *and* the SID off if I— Got it! It's working! Look,' Sally says, pressing the play/record buttons again and flashing a red light in my face. She grabs her notebook off the table. 'OK. You *do not* have the right to remain silent. Anything you say can and *will* be used against you as evidence. Oh, and *no* false confessions either.'

'OK,' I say. 'Shoot.'

'So, Braveheart Burns, school hotshot. How do you feel on the eve of the most exciting day of the football calendar?'

Here we go, then. Suppose this is my chance to put across what it feels like to be a football hero: what it's like limbering up for a game, the pre-match nerves, the tension we all share in the team, the pressure to perform, the exhilaration of scoring in front of a cheering crowd, lifting the cup for the fans, signing autographs for them all outside the players' entrance afterwards before jumping in the old MG sports car with Mel baby and shooting off to some hot new trendy nightclub frequented by famous pop stars of the female variety.

'As you know, Sally, I've got a job to do. The school's counting on me; the teachers, the supporters who—'

Sally switches the tape recorder off with a deafening click.

'For *fake sake*, Joey. Whadaya think this is? An interview on *Match of the Day*? I wanna know if ya think you'll score with all the girls after the game?'

'You what? I—'

'*Joke*, Joey. Lighten up, willya?' Sally switches the machine on again. 'So tell us, hotshot, are Ardrossan Rovers really interested in signing you up when you leave school in June?'

'I've already told you all that last week.'

'For the school paper, moron.'

So much for a quick five-minute chin-wag. I've run through what my favourite meals are in the school dining hall, revealed what my favourite pastimes are when I'm not at school (as if Sally didn't know, 'cause she's usually kicking the

124

ball around the garden with me), harped on about my favourite telly programmes with an educational value (yawn, yawn, quick time check again), favourite community service (yes, seriously).

Sally then goes on to explain that the main part of the planned two-page feature will be a narrative style profile on one page, hence all the favourite CV questions I've just answered. Seemingly, there's also going to be a little 'light-hearted' section in a 'Question and Answer' format on the facing page, where I've 'really got a chance to open up about other things.' Only Sally isn't opening up too much herself. Until she launches in with the first question, that is . . .

'Describe your ideal romantic fantasy?'

'*My what*? What's that got to do with school and football?'

Sally presses the pause button. 'I'm asking the questions here, remember.'

'What kind of—'

'I'm trying to bring out the sensitive lad beneath the football shirt.' She hesitates for a second, then goes on. 'Y'know, to show you've got a soft side beneath the big macho man image. That's my angle.'

'*Your angle*?'

'All reporters have to a have an angle, thicko. That's the first thing you learn at journalism school.'

'Oh, so you're at journalism school now?'

'I will be when I leave school. I'm gonna be a reporter for the teen mags so I can get to interview all the hot football totty like yerself. Anyway, are we doing this interview or not, Joey?'

So that's what kind of interview it is? Teen mag snog questions. They'll never print that kind of lovey-dovey patter in the school paper, and I'm tempted to tell Sally that she's wasting her time, but this is my chance to road test some of those love god techniques I've been practising. To show off some of the mature *amour* I've been secretly nurturing behind closed curtains in my bedroom when I should be doing my other homework.

'OK, Cub,' I tell her. 'What's next?'

'Whoja think you are – a dodgy politician dodging the scandal of the day? Ya haven't answered the first question yet. Describe yer ideal romantic fantasy?'

Hmmmn, could be tricky? Should I tell her about my hot beach fantasy in the Caribbean or not? Well, maybe the edited highlights . . .

'I think a relaxing beachy holiday would be romantic. Y'know, a spot of paragliding, get the old water skis out and—'

'Yer not one of those boys who go out with a girl for a week and already yer planning the summer holiday?'

'I was only—'

'*Next question.*' Sally peers at her battlefield of a notebook for a second, then picks up a pen and scribbles something down in the margin at the side of the page. She looks up. 'Can guys be "just good friends" with a girl, without trying to take things further?'

''Course they can. Look at us, Sal. We're best mates, aren't we?'

'What do you go for in a girl – looks or personality?'

'Well, I think we both already know the answer to that one. Mmmmn, Melanie Anderson.'

'Can I quote you on that?'

'Don't you dare!'

'Would you like to elaborate your answer a little, then.' Sally keeps her eyes on me. 'For instance, I know looks must attract you to alleg-edly pretty girls like Melanie Anderson, but surely it's personality that keeps you interested.'

'Aye, it's the old Barbie doll thing: a babe without a brain, perfect but plastic, sexy but silent.'

'Could I have a more printable answer, please?'

'Well, obviously personality is just as important as looks, 'cause looks fade. So what I'm looking for, darlin', is a girl like Melanie who has a personality as good as her looks.'

'What turns you off about girls?'

'When they nag and moan about everything – especially when their team gets beat. If they're like that now, you can only imagine what they'll be like years later when they turn into their mothers. And one *maw* is enough for me!'

'Have you ever been in love?'

Jeez, this is an in-depth interview all right.

'Eh, I thought we were steering clear of the Melanie Anderson questions.'

'Generally speaking, then. What do you feel like when you're in love?'

I'm not telling her how I feel. How I really feel, I mean. I mean all I can think about is Melanie Anderson these days. Every hour. Every minute. Every *second*. You only have to mention her name and I'm meeting her in my fantasy world, picking her up in the old MG sports car for another hot date down the Late Café. I can't sleep at night. I can't concentrate at school. I've got no appetite. I get nippy with my mum for no reason. No wonder I'm falling behind with my school work, about to flunk the Standard Grade exams I failed the first time.

'I thought you knew all the answers yerself, Sal?' There, that stalls the question.

'Oh, I know what it feels like to be in love. But know what? The interview is with you, Joey. So, how do you feel when *you're* in love?'

And there's me thinking I was off the hook on that one.

'Go on, Joey. I promise to edit out the pukey bits for ya. See, I'm even saving you a red neck as well. How many tabloids would do that for a hotshot star like yerself?'

128

'It's not that I don't want to answer yer girlie teen mag *snog* question . . .'

Sally sighs, rolling her eyes as she picks up her pen. 'Let's just scratch that question.' She flicks over the page of her notebook. 'What's the most romantic thing you've ever done?'

'You have to go out with a girl first before you can be romantic with her.'

'So will I just put down following Melanie Anderson home from school as your most romantic act to date?'

'Don't even think about it.'

'Have you ever had your heart broken?'

'Yes . . . and you did it to me when you told me Melanie was seeing Slimey Climie.'

'Do you ever get jealous when you're in love?'

'If you count GBH or attempted murder, then yes, I am slightly envious of Slimey Climie.'

'Somehow I don't think that wise guy answer will make the *School Voice* either. You're not very quotable, Joey. Can you try a little harder. Remember who the readers are.'

As if I could forget. I really regret doing this interview, I can tell you.

'Ah, here's an easy question. D'you remember your first snog?'

Silence.

On my side of the tape recorder.

Sally's waiting for me to speak. So am I. I mean my kisser is open – but no words are coming out.

129

'Shall I repeat the question?' She smiles shyly. *'Have ya ever tongued a girl down behind the tennis courts?'*

'I'm not telling you that! What if Jennifer Dunlop – I mean, what if everybody reads it.' No! And it's on tape, too.

'Jennifer Dunlop, eh? I know you *now*, Joey Burns. Jennifer Dunlop. My, my. Whoever would have guessed . . .?'

'That's strictly off the record, Sal. Just between you and me. You'd better not say she was my girlfriend. We only kissed once, we never even went out with each other.'

'Relax, willya.'

Except I can't. The interview goes on for another ten minutes and Sally doesn't even mention the words school, football, cup or goal.

We sit in silence listening to the rest of the tape play back, Sally smiling, me shifting uncomfortably on the edge of her bed as the action replay almost winds to an end. And it's not just because my voice sounds high-pitched and boyish on that poxy tinny Dictaphone of hers . . . that's not really *me* speaking?

'Have you ever two-timed a girl, Joey?'

'I could never do that. I'd feel too guilty.'

'Has a girl ever two-timed you?'

'Not that I know of.'

'Have you ever dumped a girl – or been dumped yourself?'

'No, in both cases.'

'How many girlfriends have you had exactly?'

'Hmmmn, I've lost count to tell you the truth.'

'Roughly speaking?'

'It's hard to say.'

'Go on, name a number. Is it one, two, ten?'

'OK, OK, Sal – you *know* I've never had a girlfriend. Are you happy now? Er, ya won't print that last bit, *willya*?'

19

On the way out of Sally's house, I suddenly remember something and turn back. 'Will you be sure to let me read the article first before it gets printed, like you promised?'

'Aye, I did promise, didn't I . . .' Sally's on the doorstep now, closing the door quietly behind her. 'Know what?' she says, her voice low. 'Time I get it typed up tomorrow I'll have to take it right over to Melanie Anderson to be edited. With the cup final at night it'll be a mad rush to get it laid out on the computer to come out on the Friday issue with Melanie's match report. See, she has to write her article on Thursday after the game, so she'll have to edit mine tomorrow.'

And there's something else I haven't forgotten either.

'What about the coaching session? You still haven't helped me with—' I start whispering, too, in case Serious Sarge is tuning in behind the lace curtains of that two-way mirror window of his – 'that other hot news story we were talking about.'

'Aye, and yer right there as well.' Sally takes

my arm and leads me up the garden path. 'Know what?' she says as we reach the gate. 'It's gonna take time. Time I got to know Melanie better. I haven't really spoken to her yet. Apart from asking her if I could interview ya. She was busy at the time putting her slap on before she went to interview Mr Lovett for the teacher of the month profile. She just told me to get on with it.' Sally pauses. 'But once she reads my sparkling prose and we become a real editorial team and hang out together, I'll be able to find out all about her for ya!'

'So basically what you're saying, Sal, is that you're putting my love life on hold till after the cup final.'

'At least.' She's opening the gate now and practically pushing me out on the street. 'Don't be dumber than dumb, *dumb*. Think about it. Ya don't want to make a move on Melanie Anderson till you've dazzled her on the pitch tomorrow night and won the cup for us. Not only will she already have read about you in my article – she'll be able to see you in action.' She shuts the gate, then grins. 'D'ya get me?'

'Oh, aye, I get you now.' I really do. What a wee schemer. 'You've got it all worked out, haven't ya?'

'Trust me, Joey. Before the week's over I'll have you practically joined at the hip with Melanie Anderson.'

When I get in the house I find my mum sitting

133

on the sofa, sifting through the pile of old photos she keeps stuffed away in the family album shoe-box at the bottom of the sideboard.

'Here, Laddie.' I stroke the wee boy's head as he scampers about at my feet. 'Down now . . . Good dog.'

'I didn't hear you come in there,' my mum says after awhile. 'I was just sorting out the photos.'

I pick up one of the pics while I stare at my mum. 'Doesn't Dad look really young in his Ardrossan Rovers strip? He was so thin, too.'

'I was just thinking that myself, son. He wasn't much older than you are now.'

'Mum?'

'Yes.'

'Do you miss him?'

'Oh, Joey, of course I do, son.' She gets to her feet and puts her arms round me. 'I know we had our problems but that doesn't mean I didn't love him.' She hugs me harder. 'You don't stop loving someone because they're dead. If you love someone long enough their memory will live on in your heart for ever. He'll always be your dad.'

We stand there for a while without speaking, my mum holding me, and I'm not even trying to get away.

'You are still coming to the cup final tomorrow night, aren't ya?'

'Of course I am, son.' She tries to smile, but she can't hide the sad look in her eyes. 'Your dad would have been there, too. He still will be, in a way. He loved Rover Park.'

When Laddie and I go up to my bedroom and I close the door behind me, I'm kind of crying. I don't know why. All the feelings I've kept bottled-up for the past few weeks suddenly come to the surface as the realisation of what has happened to my dad starts to hit me. It was seeing that old photo of him in his football strip that's set me off.

I sigh as I look over at Laddie lying in his bed. The poor wee boy's bed is just a big cardboard egg box I snatched from Safeways with the side ripped off so he doesn't have to climb in and out whenever he wants to flop down in the sack.

I look at him and say, 'I'll have to talk Maw round into getting ya one of those tartan beds from the pet shop in Saltcoats. A proper pooch pit for ya 'cause you'll never have to sleep outside in the snow again. My wee doggie boy!'

I start laughing. I'm really creasing up in a fit of giggles. Laddie knows something's up 'cause he's up and tearing into my slipper as I dangle a leg deliberately over the edge of my bed. I'm practically killing myself laughing as I watch Laddie eating my stinky old slipper I've melted halfway through the plastic sole. I'm going, 'Grrr! Grrr!' and then I'm saying 'Kill! Kill!' as he rips my slipper to pieces, pretending it's a big water rat or that fat ginger cat across the road.

'Ya wanna jump in bed with me tonight?' I tell him. 'It can't be much fun having forty winks in that old egg box, boy! My buddy boy! Wee Laddie, ya!'

Then, suddenly, my mum shouts up the stairs, 'Make less racket up there, you two. It's way past your bedtime, Joey. Try to get some sleep, son, you've got a big day ahead of you tomorrow.'

'Aye, *Maw* . . .'

I whisper to Laddie that it's all clear now and he can jump in here with me. I move over to make room for him in my bed and he nose dives right under the duvet. 'Good boy, good boy. No snoring now!' I feel him rustling about and getting comfortable and then he makes a contented doggie sigh. 'Goodnight, John Boy,' I whisper. And then I think about my dad again. John Robert Burns. May you rest in peace.

I hear my mum footering around downstairs, catching up on all her housework, no doubt; all tired and tense and dead on her feet, too. I wonder how it will go tomorrow? All I know is that it's going to be a BIG day.

I turn over in my bed again. I'm never going to sleep tonight. I'm too excited. My mind's hyper. And not only 'cause it's the cup final tomorrow. I'm in ecstasy! Love is the drug for me, all right! Me and Mel together at last! It's a cinch now with Sally on my side.

I'll have you practically joined at the hip with Melanie Anderson.

I have to play brilliantly tomorrow. I have to win us the cup. I have to score a hat-trick at least. I have to score with Melanie.

I have to sleep!

20

It's official: I'm a total hero here at school today, judging by the support that's being heaped on me by my army of loyal fans, that is. You can almost feel the buzz of excitement sweeping through the playground as the build up to the big game tonight gets under way. It's infectious. Everybody, and I mean *everybody*, is breaking out with the old back-slapping palaver.

'No matter whether you win or lose, boy, the whole school will be proud of your achievement.' – Rector Bates

'I've already filed my interview for the *School Voice*. I've told Melanie Anderson just to *watch* the hotshot in action.' – Sally

'Ya won't believe the number of girls who are going tonight – we're talkin' at *least* five-a-side *each*!' – Rab Guthrie

'Forget about the scout from Ardrossan Rovers, Braveheart, just concentrate on the game at hand.' – Love it Lovett

'You'd better waste them, Burns, or I'll waste you.' – Slimey Climie.

Which just goes to show – you can't please all the punters all the time.

That afternoon, while I'm waiting for Rab Guthrie outside the school gym, Melanie Anderson walks past me. She keeps on walking. Obviously she hasn't had a chance yet to read Sally's exclusive interview. She'll be back . . . I hope.

Rab pulls a packet of Orbit from the pocket of his baseball jacket, slumps down beside me on the grass by the tennis courts and asks, 'Getting excited, Joey boy? I know I am.'

'Nervous as hell, more like it. The whole school's counting on me, y'know.'

'Well, ya have played blindin' all season, mate.'

'It's a huge responsibility all the same.'

Rab leans over on his elbow, passes me a stick of gum. 'Don't be soft. Yur the hottest player in the Ayrshire league, boy. And it was Love it Lovett that said it, no' me.'

'It's amazing to think that he's only been here since the beginning of the year. Not even four months. The team was all over the place before he took charge. He's done a great job getting us to the final.'

'There's only one ace at our school . . .' Rab's big tennis ball eyes follow the game a pair of leggy girls have just started serving up for us on the courts. 'If we're still talkin' about football, that is!'

I laugh, lying back on the grass with my head against my school bag. Rab Guthrie and girls! I watch the clouds scudding across the darkening sky, wondering if it'll keep dry for tonight. 'It's gonna be weird, all the same, playing at Rover Park.'

'It's a pity yur faither won't be there to see ya. He would have been so proud of ya.'

I sigh. 'I still can't believe it. I still expect him to walk through the door any minute. It's as if he's still here.'

'My faither said yur dad used tae be some football player. He's passed it on tae you, all right, hotshot. Even ma faither is comin' doon with oor Mick tae watch ya play!'

'Is he really coming to watch me?'

'The whole toon is, boy!'

Apart from my dad, I'm thinking. Oh, Dad.

'It's a lot to live up to, Rab.'

'Wait till yur wearin' an Ardrossan Rovers strip, mate. Then ya'll really know what nervous means. I wish the scout was coming tae watch *me* play.'

'I just hope it doesn't affect my game, that's all.'

'What's to worry aboot there? At least yur sorted with the job ya want when ya leave school. Ma football career ends tonight at Rover Park.'

'Whadaya mean?'

'I told ya the other night there. I won't be stickin' around for any repeat performance with the Standard Grades – never mind another season in goals. Ma faither says I've had ma shot at further education, he's no' buying any of that eternal student skiving any more. Y'know he didn't want me tae stay on fur fifth year. Neither did the teachers, come tae that.'

Rab sits up slowly, arms hugging his knees, gazing way, way beyond the traffic on the road outside to the countryside in the far distance. He turns to me, this look on his face I've never seen before, his bottom lip trembling.

'My faither's already got a job lined up fur me when I leave school. You'll no' be surprised tae know that I start at the slaughterhoose in June.'

So that's why Rab lost his rag with Ben up Castle Hill the other night. I search Rab's face for a clue to what else he's trying to tell me. But, as usual, the original hardman's giving nothing away.

'At least you've got a job, Rab. Most lads will be signing on when they leave.'

'I'd rather be on the dole.' Rab lowers his eyes, scratching his stubbly chin, his hands a little shaky. 'I know somebody's got tae do the job. And it's good money, don't get me wrong.' He looks at me. 'Y'know I'm not the type tae sponge off ma old maw. Tellya the truth, I'm kind of dreading it . . .' He looks away again. 'I – I don't think I could . . .' The side of his mouth twitches, his iron mask slipping as he struggles to hold back what his face can't hide any more. 'So much fur me trying tae be a vegetarian, huh?'

'Oh, Rab . . .' Big bad Rab. What a secret softie he is beneath that bullet-proof image of his. So that's why he's been skipping his mum's Sunday roasts – a secret vegetarian, eh?

'Y'know somethin', Joey boy. When I first heard the Rovers were interested in signing ya,' he says, quickly changing the subject, 'I was really jealous.'

'Jealous? Of *me*? It's me that's jealous of *you* – ya stud!'

'I'm no' talkin' aboot snoggin' the chicks – that's just a wee sideline I've got goin' tae make school more bearable till they kick me oot. Naw, you've got the career you've always wanted.'

'I didn't know you were career-minded, Rab. I thought you couldn't wait to *be* kicked out.'

'Oh, there's a lot of things ya don't know aboot big bad Rab Guthrie. Ya'd be surprised.'

'Such as what?'

'Naw, forget I said anythin'. My gob's almost as big as yours sometimes.' Leaning over on his side, Rab chucks a pebble into the little stream that runs by the tennis courts, listening for the plunk as it hits the water.

'Go on, Rab. Don't change the subject on me again. I'm yer best mate.'

'Didja know I've always wanted tae be a painter?' Rab says suddenly.

'*Is that all*?' I laugh. 'And there's me thinking you were about to start up yer own strip-o-gram service for girlie hen night parties. Put yer name in for one of those job experience programmes at the Job Centre, ya daft moron. They teach you how to paint pensioners' houses till you get the hang of it. Then you can start up your own business.'

'I'm no' talkin' aboot painting and decorating . . . I mean an artist.'

'*You*? An *artist*?'

'Aye, *me*. Why d'ya think I stayed on at school – it wasn't just tae postpone the slaughterhoose fur another year. I'm no' that stupid. I failed most of the Standards, I know, but I got ma Art and Metalwork. That's all I wanted. I know ya need qualifications fur . . .' Rab's eyes begin to glaze over. 'I had this dream of goin' tae art school in Glasgow. I just thought that maybe—' He blinks. 'Me, an artist?' Rab hollers. 'Yur right, Joey boy. Who am I tryin' tae kid . . .?'

So *he's* the name in the frame; the mysterious Picasso-wannabe he wouldn't tell me about who did the illustrations for my story for free. And that's the hobby he was trying to tell us about up at the castle the other night.

'And you've kept it a secret from me all this time, Rab?'

'I've no' told anybody, mate. I do portraits,

143

landscapes, the lot. I've been working away secretly to myself fur a while noo. I usually go up the North Beach on ma own tae paint, y'know. It's a lot quieter than South Beach. Less chance of somebody spottin' me and givin' the game away.'

'I still can't believe it.' I'm really interested now. 'Spill, mate . . .'

'The other day I went all the way up the Big Woods, sketched the Mill Dam in the distance. Once I even carried my easel and my canvas and oil paints over the fields next tae Chapelhill Mount . . .' Rab grabs another piece of chewing gum. 'The funny part is,' he goes on, scrunching up the gum wrapper as he speaks, 'I was sitting there in the field painting this tree when all these grazing cows started crowding round me. They must have thought I was the farmer with their feed or something. They were so friendly – more scared of *me* than I was of them. They get such a bum deal when you look at the spoiled cats and dugs we keep as pampered pets.' He pauses. 'I don't mean wee Laddie 'cause I know what a hard life he had afore Sally and you rescued him fae that jerk Hunter the Punter. Aye, he's landed on his paws at last, the wee boy . . .' Rab lets the sentence trail off as he throws another stone in the stream.

'I didn't know you went painting in the countryside?' I swipe his arm away and he falls over on his side, laughing. 'I didn't even know ya had the full art kit. If ya told me you had some spare cans of spray paint for the bus shelter of my choice, I would believe ya.'

Rab sits up. 'Toleja. There's a lot people don't know 'bout me.'

'You did that one of Arran above your fireplace, didn't ya?'

It's a beautiful painting that really captures the jagged snow-capped peaks of the island's Goat Fell mountain range.

'Aye, I own up. That was ma handy work.'

'You've got talent, Rab. Ya really have. I thought yer maw bought it out of the Kyle Gallery in Saltcoats. Even Wilma Rubber Fingers said your illustrations were good. You can be an artist – you can be anything ya want. Why don'tcha apply for art school, mate?'

'Me?' Rab breaks out in a big deep throaty laugh. 'Remember, boy, this is a Guthrie yur talkin' tae. Ma faither works in the slaughter-hoose, same as his faither afore him. Mick's already been there for three years noo.' His voice becomes tense again. 'Y'know, mate, I've spent five years waiting to escape from this school. Now that it's time for them to kick me oot, I'm kinda scared, to be honest. It's a whole different ball game oot there.'

'Ya can be an artist if you really want, y'know.' I give him a friendly nudge. 'Just think of all those nude models ya get to paint in art school, eh?'

'Aye, the thought did cross my mind.' He breaks out in a grin. 'Whered'ja think I got the

145

inspiration tae be an artist in the first place. It wasn't just that painting by numbers kit Santa gave me by mistake one Christmas when what I really wanted was a PlayStation.'

I suddenly get some artistic inspiration myself. 'Want me to speak to old Wilma Rubber Fingers for ya? Remember, I've got connections there.'

'Oh aye, the old spiritual network. The Scripture's Union.'

'Aye but don't go building yer hopes up,' I tell him with a matey grin. 'She might still have the hump over that story of ours.'

Rab shrugs. 'She's actually quite a good art teacher, y'know. It was her that got me into "creating on canvas" after I got interested in art. That's what she calls it. She got me hooked on Edward Hopper. He's this very trendy American artist, famous for contemporary work yuppies go for in a big way; long dead noo, of course. Aye, old Wilma Rubber Fingers showed me the light, all right.'

'I'm gonna speak to her for ya. See if she can help wangle you a place at art school. Just wait till I tell her it was you who did the drawings!'

'Too late to enrol noo, mate. Ma name's doon for somethin' else noo . . .' Rab gets to his feet and brushes the grass off his jeans. 'Just you worry about winning that cup for us tonight.' He lets his leer linger on the courts a second longer, drooling over the two potential art models still swinging their tennis rackets and their skimpy skirts around over there.

'Only if you promise to concentrate in goals,' I say, 'and save the painting by numbers for later.'

Rab laughs and I laugh with him. Then with one last look at the *laydeez*, we leg it.

21

Long before the teams set foot on the pitch, Rover Park is packed to capacity with girls (and a few brave boys, too!) screaming, 'We want Millglen Academy! We want Millglen Academy!' Banners sway daringly aloft declaring: 'RAB GUTHRIE HAS A CUTE BUTT!' and 'BRAVEHEART BURNS'.

Rab and I can't believe it as Mr Lovett tells us again to stop gawping through the gates and go in the door to the players' entrance with the rest of the team.

I read somewhere that women's football is one of the fastest-growing team sports in Britain. But do they know about the growing number of screaming girl supporters piling through the turnstiles into football grounds now? I tell you, the girls are chanting louder than the lads here tonight.

I'm actually quite chuffed to bits with that banner saying 'BRAVEHEART BURNS'. I didn't have a chance to see who was holding it 'cause Love it Lovett had us out of the school bus and into the ground almost like one of those bouncers the boy bands have on the tour bus. I'll bet it's wee Sally Taylor who's behind it all – trying to wind me up for a laugh. I can't think who else would pull that kind of crazy prank. OK, I'm hoping it might be Melanie Anderson (i.e. the chance is as fat as Rab's *cute* butt . . . and that isn't the crack I mean!).

Well, it serves Rab right for trying to sweet talk some of the girls into getting kitted out as cheerleaders for a bit of the all-American razzmatazz before the game gets going. Especially as Rab's main stipulation was: only those with a cute butt need apply. No wonder the girls told him to butt out!

We make our way to the changing rooms to get ready.

'I love this bit the best,' Rab says. 'All those hundreds of girls screaming for ya out there and y'know ya can have any three or four ya want afterwards.'

'Go on, lads,' I urge, hanging my jacket up on the clothes peg above the bench. 'What is he?'

'*The school stud*!' comes the resounding reply.

Shouts fill the room as Rab grabs me from behind by surprise, forcing my head down in an arm-lock as I double over in his vice-like grip.

'Oh, ya big bloater!' I scream, trying to struggle free. 'Get yer B.O. outta my face!'

Rab laughs away, screwing his knuckles even harder into my head. 'Yur lucky I've no' got ma studded goalie gloves on yet! I'm saving them for the Woodside team!'

'Get him, lads!' Ronnie Cowan gives the word.

I hear a mad shuffle of feet as the team follow the captain's orders, prizing us apart and piling into Rab.

'Yur still no' any match for me,' a smothered voice calls out from beneath the pile of bodies. 'I could take ya all on with only one hand . . . and I still wouldn't need ma studded-gloves!'

We're always clowning around, having mock punch-ups, calling each other names, anything to rev ourselves up and get the adrenaline pumping. Not that we need much of that tonight. We're all as high as rock stars about to go on stage – and we're not even throwing any toilet seats out the window or anything.

And now we're running about in our undies trying to get into our blue-and-white strips. Well, Rab Guthrie is. He's the worst in kit-on *and* kit-off *strip* situations. And that's what I'm dreading the most – win or lose the cup tonight. Rover Park is a real football ground, remember, so it's got one of those big baths all the players jump into together after the game. You know, with no pants on or anything.

It's all right for the likes of Rab Guthrie. He's used to it. He's always dripping butt-naked wet from the showers in the gym at school 'cause he can never find his towel in all the steam. Sometimes I just pretend I don't need a shower at all. Usually I don't anyway 'cause I don't

150

sweat much. I just whip out the old deo and have a quick scoot and that's me – fresh again. I just don't like getting my kit off in changing rooms full stop, to tell you the truth. You've got no privacy, neither you have. That's why I hate getting changed in front of the other lads. I mean, I'll jump in the team bath no problem when I turn professional in a couple of years. But I've not even joined the junior league yet, so give me a break here, pal! And, anyway, if we win the cup we'll probably be too busy to have a bath. Time we've run round the pitch ten times for the old lap of honour, got the group photo for the winning team portrait and signed hundreds of autographs. If we win the cup.

If not, the Matey's always waiting . . . and it won't be a bottle of fun for me!

I'm still trying to get into my football shorts with my school shirt hanging over my pants to hide the unlucky colour (the kecks are *blue*, by the way, it's the neck that's *red*!). Old Lovett has already launched in with his pep talk about the tactics for the game. Good on you, sir. He's actually quite good at grabbing your attention – and distracting the others while I slip on my shorts – and getting us all fired up for the match.

'Listen up,' the coach says as an electrifying silence charges the room. 'As you know, lads, Woodside Academy won the school cup last year. They're also ten points clear at the top of the league and favourites to win the double this season.' He pulls a newspaper from his bag and holds the sports page up for everyone to see – not that we haven't read it already.

'It's not just the Woodside supporters who think they're going to win tonight,' the coach continues. 'The reporter from the *Ayrshire News* has tipped them as well.' He drops the paper in the bin. 'The smart money says Woodside – but I've got my money on you lot! I believe you can do it – 'cause I believe in you! Are you going to prove me right tonight, lads?'

'Yesssssssss, *sir*!' The sound of fourteen fired-up football players roars through the room.

I watch old Lovett talking to Rab as he goes round everyone in the team. It's funny how *sir* acts all matey – like one of the lads – when he's out of school. In the classroom it's all, 'You, boy!' and, 'Burns, wake up!' He doesn't have to tell me that this is the moment we've all been working hard for, that we know we've got a job to do . . . but I let him tell me anyway.

'Y'know we're all counting on you, Braveheart.'

'I won't let you down, sir. I won't let down the team.'

'Good, Joey. I knew I could count on you.'

I'll bet he's an all right bloke out of school. With his own mates, I mean. I'd love to know what that babe looks like that Lovett's

152

snogging. Just to see what kind of chick does the trick for him, I mean.

'Are you listening, Joey?'

Lovett's looking at me.

So are the lads.

I tell them, 'Just watch me, team, when I get on that pitch!'

Before we get on the pitch we always go through a pre-match ritual. Roland Brown-nose summed it up perfectly that time we let him be a substitute: 'If I don't get to slap hands and hug everyone I don't feel good before a game.' And he still wonders why we kicked him out the team after the match without even letting him on the pitch. In fact, there's always lots of hugging and exchanging 'Good Luck' messages before the match:

'We're in this together, team!' – Ronnie Cowan.

'Go for it!' – Tam Gibbens.

'Scud them good an' proper, boys.' – Rab Guthrie.

'Let's get out there, then, and show them!' – Coach Lovett.

'I'll be cheering you all on!' – Roland Brown-nose.

Who gave *him* the special backstage VIP pass?

Ben Robinson even has a wee personal message of his own, which he whispers to Rab

Guthrie when he thinks no one else is listening . . .

'Listen, Rab, I'm sorry for being a jerk the other night. I'm getting a bit of grief at home just now, that's all.'

'Yur faither,' Rab says. 'Forcing ya into doing something ya don't want to when ya leave school?'

'Aye.'

'I know how ya feel, mate.'

'So you tackle those Woodside lads hard,' Rab tells Ben when he sees me looking at them.

'Aye, mate, and you knuckle them harder with those studded gloves of yours!'

Rab turns, grinning, toward the rest of the team. 'Let's kill them, boys!'

The coach smiles. 'Show this kind of fighting spirit on the pitch, lads, and we'll win that cup tonight!'

Tensing now with pre-match nerves, knowing it's our last big game together as a team, we walk, studs crick-cricking, down the concrete tunnel which will take us out to the waiting crowd.

And then it's: 'Weyyyyy!!! Away the lads!!!'

22

We've had the dress rehearsal, now it's the official team photographs. As we get into position for the shot, I catch a quick glimpse of a familiar blue-and-white Nike tracksuit darting between the bods in front of us. Aye, it's wee Sally Taylor all right, trying to squeeze between the teachers and official local press photographers with that nifty new Cannon zoom lens camera. Serious Sarge probably gave it to her for her birthday, from the gift catalogue they've got down the cop shop. She shouldn't be on the pitch – no wonder she's being told to beat it and get back in with the crowd. And . . . Oh, God! *Goddess*! Melanie Anderson's walking straight towards me with a smiling Mr Lovett, her notebook and her pen poised for an exclusive interview with the man of the match.

OK, so maybe she's interviewing the team boss before the game gets going. But I'll be next. When the game's over. And I'm holding the cup victoriously!

Mel's legs are so lo-o-o-o-ng in those black trousers. And look at that slinky red top she's got on underneath her black leather jacket. I've never seen Mel out of her school uniform before. I mean, I've never really seen her out of school before – apart from when I walk by her house sometimes at night, but I'm always too scared to look in the window, so that doesn't really count.

'I see you're out of uniform tonight as well, sir,' Mel says, flirting. 'Are student teachers wearing designer labels now?'

'Aye, if suede jackets are back in again!' Rab yells over at them.

Lovett stops, then starts to laugh. 'This is supposed to be a football match – not a fashion show.'

'So where's yur trendy tracksuit, sur?'

'*Guthrie* . . .'

'Aye, sur.'

The best bit about warming-up on the pitch is pretending you're a professional footballer like it's a live game on the Sky Sports channel. None of this edited highlights and straight on with the match. I'm limbering up, swinging my arms and shaking my legs to loosen up the muscles. I've got muscles – I've got a six-pack and everything. It's just that I'm quite skinny-looking, that's all. Hotshot skinny, to give me the speed I need when I'm running with the ball. Like right now, boy! I'm running fast on the spot and knocking the ball back and forwards to the other lads in the team. I'm alive! On stage! In concert! The floodlights are dazzling above us in the dark cloudless sky – the spotlight on me! There are hundreds of people looking only at ME! Well not just me, the other players as well, but it feels like it's only *me*. I wish my dad was here to watch me play. He would have been so proud.

I glance over at Sal with her pal Morag, standing next to my mum and Laddie. I thought Sally was only joking when she said she was going to wrap a football scarf round Laddie's neck and make him the school mascot. Especially now that my maw's just bought the wee Scotland supporter that new Tartan Army collar and lead to make up for all the previous birthday prezzies he's never had. And I was right about that banner! It was Sally all along. Morag and her are holding it up between them.

'BRAVEHEART BURNS'.

I'm glad we've got a lot of home support on our side 'cause the Woodside team look a lot bigger on the pitch in their red-and-black strips. They look more like Slimey Climie and his rugby club mates who're hogging all the best seats up there in the stand.

You'd better waste them, Burns, or I'll waste you.

I'm glad old Slimeball managed to make it after all. I could really do with his support tonight.

I pass the ball to Rab in goals. 'So you can get a feel for it,' I yell.

Rab shouts back, 'I get enough feels from birds, mate.'

He holds the ball up to his face and plants a big smacker on it. 'Some of the foreign players kiss the ball 'afore the game. It's supposed tae bring them luck.'

He kicks the ball high in the air then hollers, 'Ya can all kiss ma big cute butt if ya want!'

'Thanks for the offer, Guthrie,' the coach calls out from the touchline. 'But we want to win the cup.'

Now the referee's calling over both the team captains to shake hands. And then they're tossing the coin to see which end we're playing and who's kicking off the game. It's us. Me. The centre forward. And before you know it we're in position and the referee's blowing the whistle. We're in the school history books now. Just listen to the crowd cheering.

'Here we go, here we go, here we go-oh . . .'

'Go-o-o-o-o-o-o-o-o-o-o-o-o-al!!!'

I don't believe it! The game's just started and Woodside have already got the ball in the back of the net. Their players are going crazy and the supporters on their side of the park are going mental. Was Rab Guthrie sleeping there, or what?

'Sorry, lads. They must have caught me napping.'

Oh, he was looking all right . . . at the crowd of girls behind his goals!

We're only in the first ten minutes of the match

and Woodside are all over us. Me more than any other players in our team. Old Lovett was right the other day. The Woodside centre half has got me singled out for special treatment, trying to mark me out of the game. He's a real big hairy lard-ass weightlifter type, and he's really got it in for me . . . with his studs, too!

'Ohhhhh! Ya big—'

'Watch your language, son!'

'*Me*? C'mon, ref! Tell him to watch his *body language.*'

Jumping for the ball I get another kind of header that knocks me flat on my back. Jeez, that hurt! I look up from the ground and see Lard-ass grinning away as he runs after the ball. And he's a defender! Who's defending me? I get to my feet and go after the ball, too.

Running up the wing I feel a quick tug at the back of my shirt then, Whu*uuu*p! Lard-ass has got me on the ground again.

I go for another header and get Lard-ass' elbow digging in at my side instead.

'Oi, ref!'

Old Love it Lovett's up off the bench, shouting 'C'mon, lads!' in that Chelsea supporter's voice of his. I can see Melanie Anderson in her seat near the dug out, scribbling away furiously in her reporter's notebook. Woodside are going to kill us if we don't all waken up our game.

Half-time. The score is still 1-0 to Woodside

Academy. Old Lovett's not exactly lovin' it, I can tell you, when we get back in the changing room. Sitting on the benches, the cold sweat clinging to our damp shirts, we listen as the coach asks us again, 'What's wrong with you tonight, lads?'

Then he's telling me, 'Joey, you're going to have to lose fatso there.'

My thoughts exactly. I'm tempted to say, 'But it was Sally who asked my maw to come with her. She does live with me, y'know.' But it's no joking matter. I've got to shake Lard-ass if we're going to win that cup!

'I don't want to have to substitute you now, Joey.'

I don't even hear old Lovett saying 'Don't despair, lads, the game's not lost yet', 'cause my mind's already on the second half.

Substitute? Me?

Melanie!

'I'll lose Lard-ass, sir. I'll lose him.'

'That's the spirit, Braveheart.'

Coach Lovett looks at every member of the team.

'Give it all you've got now, lads. Show them how you can really play!'

The clenched fists are infectious, like a ripple through the room. We start drumming our studs on the floor like the thunderous tattoo that beat the English back at Bannockburn. And then we're on our feet and slapping skin with each other and singing as Love it Lovett rallies the Tartan Army with *his* Sassenach-friendly signature tune: 'Oh, Flower of Scotland'.

Rab shouts, 'Ya Sassenach, yeh!'

'Not tonight, Guthrie.'

Mr Lovett punches his fist in the air.

'Scotl*aaaaaaaaaaaaand*!!!'

23

The second half gets underway and I'm away up the wing. I take two guys, pass the ball to our captain Ronnie Cowan. He passes the ball back to me and I'm through the defence with just the goalie to beat.

Thu*uuuuu*d!

'Ahh, ya . . . that was sore!' So it was. The big Lard-ass!

'Penalty!' the referee shouts.

'Yeeeees!' I shout.

The ref whips out the yellow card and tells Lard-ass, 'You're getting booked for that, big boy.'

'Yeeeees!' I shout again.

'Watch it,' the ref tells me. 'Or your name'll be in the book as well.'

'Are you OK to take the kick, Joey?'

'You bet, Ronnie. Gimme the ball.'

I place it on the penalty spot, then take a few steps back. As the ref blows the whistle, I run and *whup*! the ball straight in the net.

'Go-o-o-o-o-o-o-o-o-o-o-o-o-o-o-o-al!!!'

One each.

Eat my shorts, Woodside!

That'll teach Lard-ass.

Not for long, though. Foul! I take another bone-crunching 'tackle' that leaves me lying in agony for a few seconds. I get up again, limping into action, the crowd cheering for me. I feel like waving to them to tell them I'm all right, but I'm not that soft. I just hope that the next time Lard-ass has a go at me, my mum doesn't run on the pitch and try to stop the game. She would, too, my maw. Lucky Sally's dad's not here. He would probably run on the pitch as well . . . and arrest her for being a hooligan!

The ninety minutes are almost over and if it's a draw we'll be into extra time and maybe a penalty shoot-out if the score is still level. But I'm not hanging around for any of that. Not when I've got a cup to lift and a chick to pick up on the touchline over there!

Watch this, Mel baby! Watch the hotshot in action!

I see my one big chance when the ball comes shooting straight towards me. I run for it and I know that Lard-ass is right behind me. He'll be expecting me to stop, trap the ball at my feet, fumble to get in a good position as I turn to dribble past him, then he can zonk me unconscious. But I'm not falling flat on my back again for that old friendly game. I'm sorry to disappoint the big hairy Lard-ass, but I don't have that kind of death wish.

So, what I do is, I go racing towards the ball

and then I open my legs and let the ball go straight through.

Turning as fast as I can, I go tearing after it.

I've got at least three yards lead on the big bruiser now, who's still trying to turn his fat hairy ass round. I'm away and running. Running with the ball. Running past the remaining defenders till I've only got the goal-keeper to beat.

We're in the last minute of the match now with no more injury time left. Glancing up at the goal, I whack the ball with all I've got and . . .

'A*aaaaaggghhhh*!'

I suddenly feel this terrific pain shoot all the way up my left leg from my ankle to the bottom of my spine. And then I'm flying through the air and the whole ground is spinning around me as if I'm going to blank out. And that's when I really do blank out . . .

Well, I must have blanked out. For the next thing I know, the trainer's squeezing his sponge on me and snapping me out of the dark. Water dribbles on my face, all warm and sticky and slevery . . .

'Get that DUG off the park!' I hear the ref shouting.

'He's not called Dug,' I whisper back. 'He's called Laddie noo!' I feel the wee boy licking my face again.

'Joey, are you all right?' Sally's voice. Scared sounding. Next to me.

'Sally . . .' I try to look up, the cold damp smell of grass in my face. I roll over on to my back in agony. I can hear myself speaking and then I can't and then I feel someone shaking me awake again.

'I couldn't hold wee Laddie back,' Sally's saying, shaking me by the shoulder. 'He bolted out of my hands when he saw you going down.'

'Am I – am I down?' I try to sit up.

'Yer one goal short of a hat trick, Joey!'

'*What have I done now, Sal?*'

'You've scored the winner, ya daft moron! We've won the cup.' She puts her hand up to her mouth. 'Oh, I love—'

'Haw, hen!' the ref calls out again, only closer. 'You shouldn't be on the pitch with that DUG!'

I try to stand up but my head is still spinning. Then I hear Sally calling Laddie, and the ref saying, 'I think the boy's got concussion.'

And that's when Mr Lovett and the rest of the team crowd round me and lift me up on my feet.

'I'm all right, I'm all right,' I say, starting to feel better now. 'Have – have we really won the cup.'

'Aye,' Rab Guthrie hollers, giving me one of his big beefy bear hugs. 'Ya scored the winner in the last minute. And there was still enough time tae give the Woodside hitman the red card. The ref sent him off!'

I look across just in time to see Lard-ass walking away, hanging his head in shame towards the changing rooms. Aye, away and get in the bath, Matey! I've got ten laps of honour to do round the park!

Then we're jumping all over the place and hugging each other as the whole school invades the pitch to swarm all over us.

Rab was right about having three or four girls each!

'C'mon, Sally. Let go now. You too, Morag . . . *Maw*!'

Rab Guthrie takes his winner's medal from the town mayor, Mr McAskie, then turns to wave at every girl in the ground. I'm next as I shuffle along the aisle in the stand, still feeling a bit giddy as I go to collect my medal. That just leaves the captain Ronnie Cowan to take the cup and lift it up for the cheering crowd.

We've won the cup!

24

'There's someone here to see you,' Mr Lovett says with his big cheesy teacher's grin as he walks into the changing room with two men. Just as I'm wondering if the tall dark-haired man in the suit is a doctor or somebody to see if I'm OK, I suddenly recognise the smaller man in the black Ardrossan Rovers tracksuit with the shock of white hair. It's Wullie Watson, the Rovers' trainer. Oh, God! Before I can say anything, the suit holds out his hand and almost breaks mine.

'I'm Nick Beatty, the Rovers' scout. You played brilliant there, son. That was some goal you scored. Not forgetting the penalty kick, of course.' He pauses. 'Are you feeling OK, though?'

'Aye, Mr Beatty.'

'I'm sure you know why we're here, Joey. So I'll cut it short and let you get changed. You'll be wanting to get out of that strip and jump in the bath with the other boys.'

'Naw, it's all right. Don't worry about me. It's—'

'You've got what it takes to be an Ardrossan

Rover,' he goes on. 'We'd be delighted to sign you up for the team, starting next season. Unless of course,' he grins, 'you were planning on going straight to Glasgow Rangers.'

'Oh, mister—'

'No, son. You get in that bath there. Wullie here can drop the contract in at your mum's house through the week.' He pauses again. 'I think Wullie wants to say a wee word as well.'

'Hello there, Joey.' Wullie Watson shakes my hand. 'Great game, boy. Your dad told me you had talent, and he was right. I trained him myself, y'know, when he was your age. I know he was playing for another team near the end, but he was proud of you, son. And I'll be proud to train you, too.'

'Oh, thanks Mr Watson. I'll not disappoint you . . .' Like my dad did, I'm thinking, and I can see it in Wullie Watson's face there for a second, too. 'I'll not let you or Ardrossan Rovers down.'

'Go on, then . . . what'ya waiting for,' Wullie Watson says. 'Get in that bath before the water gets cold.'

I wish people would stop telling me to get in that bath. Why do you think I'm pretending I'm still feeling weak. Why don't they ask Mikey Parker or Davie Wilson or Tam Gibbens. They're still hanging around, fumbling with their boot laces, pulling the old trusty deo trick. Well, maybe not Tam Gibbens 'cause he's a real stinker. I'm tempted to get in the bath just to *feel* clean. Tempted.

'There's someone else here to see you,' Mr Lovett says, and gives me another kind of grin. Don't tell me he fancies my maw? Well, who else could it be to make sure that I'm OK and I'll get home all right . . .

'Hello, Joey. Or should I say . . . man of the match?'

'M-M-M-*Melanie*.'

Goddess! She looks even more gorgeous up close and personal. No wonder all the other guys are gawping at me through the shower curtain that blocks off the bath, hollering, 'Whoo! Whoo! All right, darling?'

'Enough of that, boys,' Mr Lovett says. 'Have you never seen a girl before?'

'Not in our steamy changing room!' shouts a big deep voice. You don't have to tell me which ginger plukey stud the girls love so much is hiding behind the shower curtain. The shower curtain that's supposed to give you privacy like the shower curtain in the gym at school. Only once you get in there without your pants on, boy, you've got no privacy at all!

'C'mon now, Guthrie. Less of that,' Mr Lovett says. So he recognises Rab's laddish *Sun* reader's voice as well.

Melanie giggles. 'Now I know I shouldn't really be here. But Mr Lovett said it would be OK to have a wee quick word with you.'

'With – with me?'

169

'Of course. You're the man of the match. I'd like to interview you for the *School Voice*.'

'*With me*?' Rab says in this not-so-deep wind-up voice. 'I'll give you a revealing in-depth interview, darlin' . . .' The scud soprano suddenly drops gear into a big bass roar. 'Jump in the bubble bath, *Matey*!'

'Boys!' Lovett shouts. Good on you, sir. You tell them. Have they never seen a reporter interviewing a footballer before? OK, a goddess chatting up a love god, 'cause that's what she's doing all right. I can't get a word in – or a word out. I'm stunned speechless.

'You're so modest,' Melanie says, smiling.

Smiling.

At me!

With those beautiful babe-blue eyes. Oh, and she's got tiny little freckles speckled on the bridge of her nose. How cute! I love her even more.

'Perhaps we can hook up tomorrow at school,' she says. 'If that's all right with you?'

If it's all right with me? She's doesn't even have to ask!

'Whatever time's good for you,' I say. 'I'll be there!

'Drop into the *Voice* office then, during the morning break.' Then Melanie turns to leave. 'I know you're waiting to jump in the bath with the other boys, so I'll be popping off now.'

'We can do the interview now, if ya like. I can always wait and have a bath at home.'

'Tomorrow's fine,' Melanie says, stepping away. 'See ya, then.'

'It's a *date*,' I tell her. Well it is for me. My first date with Mel baby!

At the door she pauses. 'Well done again, hero.'

Hero? *Goddess*! She's even got a wee pet name for me already.

And then my mum really does turn up – just when I least expect her to (i.e. as usual). Sally and Laddie are right behind her, too. Hey, hang on a minute here? I know I'm supposed to be one goal short of a hat-trick . . . but I thought Sally had already interviewed me for the *School Voice*?

'You almost stole the match there yourself,' Melanie says to Sally in a snotty sort of voice as she leaves. 'You should keep that dog of yours on a lead instead of a football scarf.'

'Get a good interview?' Sally asks in another kind of voice I know only too well.

What's going on here, girls?

25

'She spiked my interview, Joey, that's what happened!'

It's five past nine and wet and we're already late for my hero's welcome at school as Sally stomps along the street, those knuckle-white fists of hers beating at the bag over her shoulder. She stops again and screams, 'She pulled my article! Deleted my disk! Cancelled my career! My days as a journo are over, Joey. And all because of that bitch!'

'There's obviously been a mistake. Some kind of mix-up,' I say, trying to sound sympathetic. I am – I really am – but the rain's getting heavier, time is racing on . . . my hero's hairdo will be ruined in a minute!

She's almost crying now. That shows how hard she's taking it, how crushed she must be. Luckily the streets are empty, I'm thinking, 'cause I've never seen her as worked up as this before.

'Oh, stop shouting and get a grip,' I tell her, hoping that she'll snap out of the mad hysterics show before we get to school.

She stops all right – but not shouting.

'There's no mistake!' She stares me straight in the face. 'The bitch spiked my story. *My* story! I spotted your talent first, Joey.'

So I shout, 'We're late for school and getting soaked because of you!'

That's put a sock in it. For a second or two anyway. Oh, I don't mean to be mean to her but she's really starting to bug me now. OK, maybe I shouldn't have told her that Melanie Anderson is interviewing me this morning. But I couldn't help it. I was dying to tell her. And I'm dying to tell everybody when I get in class, too! I mean, I tried to tell Sally last night, on the way home after the game. But I couldn't get a word in with my mum talking away non-stop, asking if my leg was all right and my head wasn't sore. No wonder Sally beat it straight into her house when we got there. Usually she hangs around with me after school matches to run through the action replay, giving me her expert analysis and comments and a quick punter joke or two. I thought that was the reason why she came in for me this morning, 'cause usually we make our own way to school with our own mates. I didn't know it was going to be a different kind of action replay she'd be playing; and in slow motion, too.

'I could have forgiven her for pulling my story,' Sally says, opening the umbrella she's had in her bag all this time. You're supposed to bring it out when it starts raining – not when you're soaked. And boy, are we dripping!

173

Shows how much she's been distracted. 'I could have forgiven her, Joey. But when I saw her moving in on you last night with her note-book and pen I knew what her game was. She's trying to steal all the glory. My story!'

Sally holds the umbrella towards me, offering to share some flower-patterned protection. A bit late now, I'm thinking as I squelch my fingers through my new wet-look wig. My hair's damaged all right, but it better not turn into a perm when it dries. Aye, I could cry, too, Sal. I've just done an hour's work-out on my wig for the most important interview of my life.

I hold the brolly for Sally anyway, but only because I'm a gentleman. I've even got my arm round her waist for support, the way you see sad couples doing in rainy cinema queues. But only to hold us together or she'll end up walking one way and I'll be away the other. I'm telling you, we're practically joined at the hip here and Sally's still shouting about the girl I *should* be Superglued to. Only she's shouting right in my lughole now.

'I could have killed her when she spiked it!'

'Well, we both know you've got the killer punch, champ.'

Sally digs a sharp girlie shoe in my shin.

'Ouch! That hurt.'

'Not as much as I'd like to hurt someone else.'

'She's only doing her job.'

'You mean I wasn't doing mine?' Sally asks accusingly.

She stops again. But *I'm* holding the brolly.

'You're only a cub.' I give her a big shove with *my* knuckles in *her* back. 'It's your first interview, for godsake.'

'Can't you see what she's up to? She's pulling rank on me.'

'She's not up to anything.'

'Oh, she is.' Sally eyes me. 'She's trying to move in on my man of the match. And you can't even see it.'

'It's only an interview.'

'Not with me it isn't.'

'It's not my fault she spiked it!'

Another silence. Only the pitter-patter of rain on the brolly.

Finally, we get to school. I step out from the shelter of Sally's umbrella and hand it back to her. The rain's easing off now, but Sally's not as she closes the dripping brolly and gives it a good old soggy shake over my shoes.

'We're here now,' I tell her. 'You know the school rules as well as I do.'

And the most important rule for me is that we have to pretend we don't know each other. We might be neighbours. We might be best friends. We might be partners at football practice. We might even have the occasional little tiff, like we've just had now. But once we're through that gate, mate, she's third year and I'm fifth year. She's a third-year girl, I'm a fifth-year boy. We've got appearances to keep up with here, you know. It's OK to give each other a quick nod in the corridor or say hello if we happen to pass each other in the playground. But once we're through that gate together, there's no more *together*. It just doesn't happen. I mean, Sally would look ultra-cool with the girls in her class, I'll bet, if she was seen to be matey with me; but I would get a right slagging off the lads in my year if they knew or even suspected I hung out with a third-year girl. Not even Rab Guthrie would go out with a third-year girl and he goes with any girls. Actually, Rab's not even into fifth-year girls any more but always chasing after what he calls, 'sixth-year skirt'. And the sixth-year girls actually go out with him – even though he's a year younger. I swear to God. But basically, there's no way we're bouncing the ball with third-year girlie girls. And that's it. End of story.

'You go first,' I tell Sally. 'See ya later, mate.'

'Aye, and don't forget to tell the bitch I was asking for her.'

'Sally.' I go to grab her arm.

'No, forget it. Just leave me alone.'

She pulls free and splashes through the puddles in the empty playground. While I'm standing there, gazing up at the school to see if anybody's got binoculars at the windows, she's swinging the door open and slipping inside the building.

26

The *School Voice* office is just a converted class-room really, with three or four 'news desks' spaced evenly apart; a couple with computers plonked on top; lots of books, files, paper lying scattered all over the place. Well, that looks like the set-up . . . from what I can make out through the frosted glass window in the wood-panelled door.

When I finally pluck up the courage to go in the room, I find Melanie Anderson waiting for me. Alone. Conveniently alone. For her – as well as for me? Melanie . . . ya know you don't have to impress me, darlin'. I know you're a wee conscientious hard worker who deserves all those A marks. Just look at the lass with her gorgeous blonde head stuck in that pile of paperwork on her desk, scribbling away furiously like the swots when teachers fire the starting gun for exams. She's running the whole show, if you ask me, while everybody else is skiving away on the tea break. Eh, Mr Lovett? Eh, sir?

Oooh, she's so posh looking – even in her school uniform. Bet that blue blazer draped over the back of the chair has a designer label, too. I could act posh as well, you know. I know all the brand names to buy. If I had posh dosh, I mean.

She hasn't spoken yet. Neither have I, though. Maybe she never heard me open the door. Well I am tip-toeing over in case I disturb her concentration. OK, I'm creeping 'cause I'm trembling inside. That's also why I'm keeping the flow of lurrve talk low, sloooow. Boy, is she concentrating! She's still pretending I'm not even in the room as she jots down some extra questions for the only hotshot football hero we both know – who shall remain nameless, until his name is in print in the school paper, that is. Well I'm sorry, Mel baby, but I'm not hanging around here waiting for you to make the first move. I'm not hiding how I feel, even if you are.

'It's me! I'm here!' I feel like shouting – only she beats me to it.

'You're early,' she says, not even looking up from her desk. How did she know it was me? Of course, silly me, how modest can a real man be. It's my body language that's doing the talking for me. I almost forgot about it there for a moment. Subconsciously, though, I'm being as seductive as a love god's stare across a crowded dance floor. Making it impossible for her to resist *temptation*. Let me put your mind at ease, *cherie*, as I ease myself slowly into the seat in front of your desk.

'Am I really early?' I say, pretending I'm shy,

178

but letting her know, subtly, sensually, how mean and keen I really am.

'I'm just finishing off my match report, Joey, won't keep you a moment.'

She suddenly looks up from the jumble of papers on her desk and I almost jump out my seat.

'Don't looks so nervous,' she laughs. 'It's only a wee interview.'

'I'm not nervous, I'm not,' I splutter in my high-pitched voice, my hands gripping the sides of the seat as if I'm on the Nemesis ride at Alton Towers. Like *right*. I'm very calm at the moment, as a matter of fact, and way too cool for any of that dork-dweeb-nerd-geek routine. So I just smile back without even speaking. So I don't disturb her, I mean.

'Ya almost finished?' I ask after a while.

Mel looks up as I look away. 'I haven't even started with you yet.' I hear her giggling as I gaze out the window. 'You've got nothing to worry about, Braveheart. I promise to be very gentle with you.'

I spin round but her head is down again.

Oh, goddess! I've died and gone to heaven. Say those words again, *cherie*. Caress my fragile confidence, please. They might be sweet nothings to poncey poetry lovers but Mel baby can whisper that kind of lurve talk in my direction anytime, pal.

Oooh, I love the way the corner of her mouth

179

creases when she's concentrating. And the way her brow furrows almost like a frown. And the way the sunlight catches her gorgeous soft blonde hair.

'*Phew*, it's hot in here . . .' I say, my hand blocking out the sun streaming through the wall of glass facing us. 'Unbelievable after all that rain we had this morning. I got soaked – did you? Here, lemme open a window for ya.' I get to my feet, accidentally screeching the seat on the wax-buffed floor as I push it back. Ooops!

Melanie's head shoots up in alarm.

'Don't, Joey. Please don't. The playground gets so noisy in the break.'

'*Sorry*,' I whisper. '*Won't speak again.*' Ooops! I sit down, my eyes not leaving hers, even when she looks away and carries on scribbling.

This isn't working out the way I had it planned. When I was dreaming about it in bed last night, I mean. I'm not projecting the right cool image here. But I spent hours working it out over and over again 'cause I couldn't get to sleep.

'I might be a while yet, Joey.'

No, don't say that. Don't ask me to leave.

'Carry on, Mel. Don't mind me.'

Am I trying too hard? Is that it? Oh no, I forgot: you have to be mean to keep them keen. Right, she can make all the moves from now on.

'There's some back issues of the *Voice* over in that far corner.' She points way, way over the other side of the classroom. 'Flick through

180

them if you like. Get the slant of the interviews. What kind of questions I'll be asking you.'

I'm not moving that far away. I've just got here.

'I've got all the back issues at home, actually.'

There, that's let her know how much I like and follow her work. I must be back in her good books now. So why's she giving me that funny look again?

'My collection,' I say, though I'm sure she knows *exactly* what I mean. 'I've got all your interviews at home, Mel.'

Oh no, she doesn't think I meant I cut all her articles out and paste them in a scrapbook, does she? Well, I do. Well, I have done. But only the ones with her picture, like when she got to meet that minister from the Church of Scotland and when she interviewed some career's officer from the Royal Bank of Scotland. But there's no way I'm owning up to that one.

'Look, Joey, let's just do the interview now. I can finish this off later. And at least it'll be over and done with.'

Yes!

'Ready when you are, Mel.'

Boy, I didn't know I could be sooo *seductive*. She can't wait. Look how hot and flustered she's getting and I haven't even given her my sensual stare yet. And there was me worrying for nothing. For nothing! Phew. I'm such a worrier, so I am. See? I'm even worrying about worrying now!

181

'I'm a wee bit confused,' I tell Mel before she switches on her Dictaphone. 'I thought Sally Taylor – your new cub reporter from third year – had already done an interview with me.'

'Oh, that.'

That? That?

'She really should have checked with me first, y'know. She doesn't have the experience yet to write main interview features. Sally's a lovely girl, don't get me wrong. And she's very keen to learn. But we usually have cubs checking spelling, making tea for Mr Lovett. That sort of thing.'

'Was it not very good, then?'

'Oh, it was good. I enjoyed reading it. She has a very vivid imagination. She's actually quite a good wee writer.'

Then Melanie starts explaining how the type and style of interview was more like the gossipy-type that teen mags print and 'not at all suitable for an academic publication' like the *School Voice*.

'So you see, I had to spike it. It was far too racy. Rector Bates wouldn't go for that sort of chatty style. But give the girl credit where it's due. She did manage to bring out a hidden side to you. I feel I know everything there is to know about you.'

Is that good or bad? You bet Sally's brought out a hidden side to me. I knew she was getting too nosey with those snog questions. Now Melanie knows all my sad lad secrets.

182

'I'll probably use some of the info for a little fact file – giving Sally a byline, of course. Favourite subjects at school, biographical details like date of birth, hobbies, star sign. Oh, and you saving that poor wee dog's life. That's the kind of good human interest angle that makes a page really come alive. Sally does have a natural journalistic instinct for a good news story. Give her another term or two and she'll soon be sitting in my seat.'

Aye, darlin', 'cause by that time you'll be too busy sharing a sofa with me in my new lad pad!

Just as Melanie's about to give me her full undivided attention, the Editor-in-Chief bounds in. Old Love it Lovett's got better timing than my maw!

'Thought I'd find you here, Melanie . . .' He seems a little surprised to see me. 'Ahh, how's the hero this morning? Well done again, Joey. You made us all proud last night.'

I'm glad he remembers. It was *me* who scored the goals, you know.

I sort of glance away from Melanie's gaze for a second, so Mr Lovett doesn't think I'm totally ignoring his hero worshipping. Then, when I look back to watch Mel swooning at my feet, I hear Mr Lovett say, 'Listen, Melanie, I'm just on my way into a quick staff meeting . . .'

Don't stop now, sir! Sure, Melanie knows I'm the hero, that's why I'm here. But coming from a teacher . . . I need your stamp of approval. Tell her how I'll probably join

183

Kilmarnock after a season or two with Ardrossan Rovers then transfer down to Manchester United. Tell her, sir. Sir!

'. . . a quick staff meeting about the school party tomorrow night for fifth and sixth year. The board are all behind me on it – we're all in agreement that it's a terrific reward for winning the cup. Sorry, but we'll have to get a small piece in the issue for tomorrow; to let all the senior pupils know.'

Paaaarty! Wait till I tell Rab!

'I don't mind staying on over lunch, sir.' She twinkles. 'I've brought another wee packed lunch with me again.'

'I knew I could count on you, Melanie. Must dash. I'll pop in later.'

What a secret teacher's pet she is. I'll pretend I never heard that one, Melanie. I'm prepared to forgive her, though. But only because I'm going to pull her at the party. Oh, I love how those dimples crack open in her cheeks when she smiles. They're sooo cute. OK, I know I'm a pure puke – but I don't care! Paaaarty!

'I can stay and help if ya like.'

Double puke!

'It's all right, Joey. Let's just do the interview.'

27

The interview with Melanie, when it finally 'happens', is nothing at all like the girlie questions Sally grilled me with. It's all career plans, further education, aspirations for the future. The funny thing is, although the interview is supposed to be with *me*, we somehow always end up talking about *her*.

'It's not easy being the most popular girl at school,' Melanie says, even before I can tell her what it's like to be the most-talked about person in school today. She doesn't have to explain her babe appeal to me. I've seen the way all my mates drool over her, too.

Then, when Mel tells me old Love it Lovett plans to present the cup again to the team during the school party, she tells me it was her idea to ask all the teachers to club together for a going-away present for Mr Lovett 'cause he's leaving school tomorrow.

'Tomorrow? Mr Lovett?'

'His teaching placement has finished now, Joey. Didn't you know?'

'But he hasn't even been here four months.'

185

'He's only a student teacher, remember. He's going back to college next week.'

'I thought he'd be hanging around here till the end of term. Or at least till after the exams are finished.'

'Y'know he doesn't teach any specific subject. Only covering and filling in for other teachers. That's why he had time to start up the *School Voice* and coach the football team. He has his own exams to sit, too, y'know.'

'It's a bit sudden!' I still can't believe it. I'm completely blown away!

'He was supposed to go back sooner, y'know. But he asked the college if he could stay on here for the cup final. He knew how much it meant to you boys.'

'He never told us – and we're in his team.'

'He probably wasn't allowed to say anything. You know what teachers are like.' Melanie smiles. 'Don't worry, everyone will know tomorrow when they read my Teacher-of-the-Month interview with Mr Lovett in the *Voice*. You *will* promise to keep the news about him leaving to yourself, Joey. I don't want it spoiling my exclusive for tomorrow.'

'You know you only have to ask me once.'

And while we're on the subject of fond farewells, Melanie suddenly drops the bomb-shell that she's planning to go to college in Glasgow, too.

'Same with me,' I tell her. 'I'm thinking of moving up there as well.' And then I start telling her how I might play for Celtic or Rangers or Partick Thistle if I'm really stuck. I'm lying my head off, of course, 'cause there's only one team I'll be playing for after I get a bit of practice in with Ardrossan Rovers – and that's Ayrshire Killie, pal. I don't know why I'm lying, to tell you the truth. I even believe it myself.

Melanie's staring at me again so I kind of flick my hair away from my face. I do that a lot when people are looking at me and I'm lying my head off. Usually I hate my thatch 'cause it's always flopping over my face like straw. It kind of covers my smiler a lot, which is good, I suppose, when you're lying your head off.

'I thought you had your heart set on joining Kilmarnock?' Mel asks me. 'That's what it said in Sally Taylor's interview.'

'Aye, they'll probably want me as well. It's a difficult choice, you know. But Glasgow's a bigger city, where it's all happening.'

And then there's the moment in the interview when Melanie really brings out the hidden self in me. When I end up interviewing *her*!

'Suppose you'll be going to the party with William Climie, then?'

'Whatever gave you *that* idea?'

'I thought you two were an item?'

'Oh, I'm with you now. You mean that unfortunate little incident that took place in the playground the other day with Mr Lovett.'

'Aye, it was a right ruck. I was ready to jump in for ya, y'know.' So she'll know.

'You're not just a hero on the pitch, then.' She twinkles at *me* now. 'If you must know, William and I did go out on one or two little dates. Nothing serious, though. There's no man in my life just now.'

'You don't? You? But—'

'I'll probably just go to the party with Lucy Harper and the girls.'

Oh, I'd love to take you to the party, Mel. Just me and you, darlin'.

'It's really nice of you to ask, Joey.'

'What?'

'I'd love to go with you.'

Me and my big gob!

Yesss!!!

'Are ya – are ya serious? Yer not just winding me up, now?'

'I said I'd go with you. Unless you don't want to?'

She *looks* serious.

'Where'dja wanna meet? Name a time, a place. Your house? I'll pick ya up. Or we can meet somewhere. Anywhere. I'll be there. Just tell me the time, the place. I'll be there, I'll be there . . .'

I can't wait to tell Sally I've scored. And without even needing any real coaching lessons off her really. I mean, I'll pretend it was with her help and advice and that. I don't want to sound ungrateful 'cause she did try to fix me up with Melanie. But I've done it on my own! I've scored! I've pulled! And I don't care who gives me weird looks as I race out of the *School Voice* office and along the corridor.

I'm the male who cannot fail!

28

'But she said she'll give you a byline for using part of your article as a fact file.'

'I don't care.'

'I thought you'd be pleased for me, Sally.'

And I thought the brilliant news would cheer her up after the way she was acting this morning. But she's worse than ever now.

'I don't care, Joey. Can't you see that?'

'Is it the party? Is that it? I told you it's a combined one for fifth and sixth year only. It's not my fault you're not allowed to go.'

'It's not that. Listen, Joey, have you forgotten that you're breaking your other school rule here? This is the playground. People can see us. You're only supposed to say a quick hello before you pretend you hardly know me.'

Which is pure dork talk, by the way, 'cause I've grabbed her over by the gate and most people are still in the dining hall having lunch.

'Sally . . .'

'Save it, Joey. Go find another goalkeeper to bounce the ball with.'

'C'mon, Sally.'

'Look, I'd better go.'

'You're always saying, "I'd better go".'

'Aye, well this time I mean it. Permanently.'

'Sally . . .'

'Stop saying Sally. It's Melanie now. You've got the girl you've always wanted. You don't need a substitute hanging round with you any more. Soon you'll be joining Ardrossan Rovers and – there's Morag.' Sally waves over at her pal. 'Be with ya in a minute!' She turns back to me. 'Look, Joey. I'm happy if you're happy. I am, really I am. But I just think it's best if we have a break from each other.'

'I thought we were the home team.'

'We were the home team. Now you're playing with your dream team . . . and I'm playing away.'

'Whatja mean?'

'It's not just for you, Joey. It's for me, too. I've got my exams coming up and we're going on holiday early this year, in July.'

'But Serious Sarge always takes the beginning of August off before you go back to school.'

'I might not be going back to school. This school anyway.' She looks me straight in the eyes. 'You may as well know 'cause I didn't know how to tell you earlier. My dad's been offered a transfer down to Dumfries.'

'Dumfries?'

'It's better money, more responsibility. Even my mum said he'd be crazy to pass it up. He comes from that area, remember?'

'But your mum comes from here. *You* come from here.'

'I'm just the daughter. I don't have a vote.'

'Dumfries?' I say again.

'I know. It's almost over the border, but not quite. We'll still be in the real Scotland Yard. Hey,' she gives a half smile, 'at least Dumfries is nearer Manchester when ya transfer to United. Or Liverpool if ya want to join a winning team.'

'You're not really going away . . . leaving?'

'This isn't easy for me either, Joey. Why do you think I was so upset this morning? I've only just found out myself. My mum didn't want to tell me at first.' Sally waves over at Morag again. 'Look, it's not fair on her. She's waiting for me. I've got to go.' She touches my hand softly. 'And this time I really am going. G'bye, Joey.'

And she goes. And I watch her go. And a part of me goes with her.

Just a minute ago I was ecstatic and now I feel deflated and depressed.

Sally looks back and catches my gaze, and then I glance away.

'We need to talk,' Sally whispers over the phone.

Then the line goes dead.

Only the connection hasn't been cut just yet . . .

'C'mon, Joey, don't give me a rubber ear. There's something I need to tell you.'

192

'I thought what we need is a break from each other.'

OK, so I'm pretending to be in the huff with her. Well, she was in the huff with me first, wasn't she? She's always getting sulky on me now. So now I'm getting sulky on her.

'It's important.'

'It's also Thursday night, Sal. My favourite TV show is on in a minute. Y'know I never miss it.'

Now *she's* not speaking.

She's not even whispering.

But I can hear breathing.

'OK, I've still got a couple of minutes. Give me the quick edited highlights.'

'Not over the phone,' she says, still whispering.

It must be important.

'Is somebody there?' Now it's *me* who's whispering.

'Aye.'

'Is he used to yer 999 calls.'

'Aye.'

'Don't tell me: he's tall, got dark hair and carries handcuffs . . . oh, and he's also trained in unarmed combat for domestic situations.'

'Funny.'

'Is he tuning in on a police wavelength?'

'*Joey*!' She's not whispering now.

'OK, then. C'mon over. But I'm taping the show first.'

29

Home Alone. My mum's not back from the shops yet. I had the house all to myself there. Now Sally's buzzing at the front door bell and Laddie's scratching at the back door to get in 'cause he can hear her, too. It's weird to think that it's only been a week since Sally was dragging me out to the pound to save Laddie. So much has happened between us since then and I don't even know what changed or when it happened. I'm glad she's here, actually. I still have that cold empty feeling she left me with when she said she was leaving. But she didn't say it was definite, did she? The Taylors have been next door since . . . since as long as I can remember.

I'm glad Laddie's there to jump all over Sally 'cause there's something weird going on between us since we had that ruck earlier today. Nothing bad, just an awkward, uncomfortable feeling like you've met a friend you haven't seen in years and you find you've got nothing in common any more. Which is weird 'cause Sally's still her same smiley self. But something has changed and we both know it and we're both pretending that everything is the same as it was before. She's not even got her tracksuit and trainers on. Just black jeans, new strappy sandals that I haven't seen her in before, a blue T-shirt and a tiny cardigan.

'Yoo, hoo! You two!'

I hear the familiar voice calling halfway down the road and for once I'm glad of her perfect timing.

'Hi, Maw,' I shout. Then I say to Sally, 'We'd better go up to my room if it's that important. Let me help my mum with the shopping bags first.'

'Here, Laddie,' Sally says as she picks the ball up off the grass and plays with the dog who's still hers, too.

'My room's a bit of a mess at the moment,' I tell Sally as I open the door and try to hold her back for a second while I grab some T-shirts off the bed and a pair of stinky socks I've just spotted on the floor. 'I usually make my own pit up in the morning. But there's not much point in doing it when you get home 'cause you'll soon be jumping back in again.'

'If boys were meant to have tidy bedrooms, they wouldn't need mums, would they?' Sally straightens the quilt on the bed while I chuck the clothes in the bottom of my wardrobe.

'Aye, yer right there,' I say, feeling the tension ease away between us. 'If my maw wasn't there to do the cooking, I'd have to eat takeaway food

195

for the rest of my life – or I'd probably starve to death.'

I don't really mind about eating loads of take-away food, you know, 'cause once you've been eating your mum's home cooking for years, all you really want is a quick kebab/curry/burger. Now that McDonald's are starting to serve up everything I'll not even have to go anywhere else by the time I get my own gaff.

'It's ages since I've been up here, Joey. What, six months, more?'

'I don't invite that many people up. It gets kinda small when there's more than one person in it.' I nudge her jokingly. 'I apologise now for my body language if I accidentally bump into ya later.'

'Is this wee Laddie's bed?' Sally says, bending down and smoothing out the blanket.

I grin. 'Ya mean the egg box that's half-chewed and falling to bits.' Don't think I never saw that wee smirk on her face.

It's not a bad room, actually, my padded cell. Once you get over the solitary confinement prison feeling those closed curtains give you. I mean I've got my own TV and video player on top of the desk, CD player on the middle shelf of the small bookcase that has more videos than books, speakers fixed to shelf brackets on the wall above. It's only temporary accom-modation, really, till I get my own lad pad.

'Some things never change,' Sally says, picking up a copy of a football mag from my desk then dropping it down again. She's always picking my stuff up. 'Another new poster, eh?' Her arm sweeps the whole room.

If you think Sally's walls are plastered with posters, you haven't seen mine yet. Babe City! Well you need something to make homework more bearable, don'tcha? I'm surprised Sally's not slagging me off more about my lurve pit, the way I'm always ribbing her about her fantasy chamber, but I can see she's got her eyes on something else.

'Go on, lemme have a look in yer wardrobe. Show me what trendy togs you've been buying now.'

'Naw.'

'C'mon.'

'I said *naw.*'

Only Sally's got the wardrobe door wide open now.

'Yer not still wearing *this*,' she says selecting anything at random, without even looking, I'll bet, as she rattles her way along the coat hangers. 'I thought I told ya to give this old tee to the charity shop. Oh, is this a new CK tee!'

'Yes it is, actually.' She's getting my sophisticated stranger in a dark corner stare for that. That'll teach her to suggest my T-shirts are the kind you snap up for a good cause at a bargain price.

'Don't tell me, Tracy Guthrie brought it back from some black market stall in Turkey or something.'

'It's a real one, if ya don't mind.' I go to grab it. 'C'mon, now. Gimme it, Sal.'

She swipes it away from me. 'Lemme borrow it. I'll give ya it back. I promise.'

Now she's getting all girlie gigglish on me, measuring the T-shirt against her for size. I knew that bringing her up to my room was a BIG mistake.

'C'mon, now, leave my new CK alone. I want it clean for the party tomorrow night.'

That stops her dead in her tracks. She slowly puts the 'tee' back on the hanger with a resigned look on her face. She's obviously just remembered that I've got the hottest date – and she's too young to go.

'Joey, that's why I had to see you, actually.'

'Oh, no! Y'know I can't get you a ticket. It's only for fifth and sixth year.'

'It's not that. It's William Climie.'

'Old Slimey?'

'And his team of rugby pals.'

'Sorry, you've lost me.'

'I heard them talking about you at school. They're going to take you after the party.'

'Me? Are you sure? Apart from that little run-in with Slimey in detention, I don't really know him that well. He's in sixth year, remember?'

'You're going with Melanie Anderson, aren't you?'

'Oh, I see. It's that.'

'Aye, *that*. He thinks you're the boy Melanie was two-timing him with.'

'*Melanie was two-timing Slimey*? But I caught *him* snogging Sarah Maloney behind the tennis courts!'

'I don't think you should go. He'll kill you.'

'I'm not scared of Slimey Climie – or his scrum of rugby jockstraps.'

'Well, I'm scared. For you, Joey.'

'Rab Guthrie'll be there to back me up again, like he did in detention.' I flex my pecs for Sal to show her I'm a real man. 'Not that I need Rab 'cause I can handle myself. I'm not worried.'

I *am* worried, though. And not just about Slimeball. Who else has Melanie been seeing?

'I'm serious, Joey. And so is William Climie.' Her voice tightens. 'D'you have to go?'

'C'mon, now. Don't get worked up.' I slip my arms round her and give her a big brotherly hug. 'Are you sure you're not exaggerating?'

'I heard them, Joey.' She shoves me away. 'They said, "We'll jump him outside and kick his face in." You're going out with his girlfriend, aren't you?'

'Ex-girlfriend, Sally.'

'Well he obviously doesn't see it that way. D'you have to go?'

'I want to go. Even if I wasn't taking Melanie, I'd still have to go. Mr Lovett's laid on a special presentation for us winning the cup. I can't let the team down. And Melanie's got a farewell surprise lined up for him because he's leaving. Sally, this is the biggest night of my life. They're

199

not spoiling my dream date. I'm going now just because of that.'

'You won't do anything crazy, will you?'

'It's not me who's making the threats. And, anyway, who told Slimey that I'm taking Melanie to the party?'

'The whole school knows about your hot date tomorrow night. It's all everybody's talking about.'

I'm glad Sally's warned me about Slimey Climie. At least I'll be prepared for any aggro at the party now, and I can try to keep out of the big bruiser's way. That fighting talk has helped clear the air between Sal and me and now we're closer than ever.

'Don't look so worried, Joey.'

I wish girls would stop saying that to me.

'Look, Joey, if you've definitely got yer big stupid crazy heart set on going to the party, then there's a few girlie ground rules you'll need to know about dating. The coaching lessons don't end just because you've got yer first date, y'know. There's a couple of "do's" and "don'ts" you still need to know.'

'Ya sure you don't mind, substitute?'

'I meant what I said, Joey. All I want is for you to be happy.'

'So, make me happy.'

Sally grins. 'OK, we know yer wearing that CK tee I let ya borrow from me.'

'It's—'

'And I'm prepared to let ya wear yer new

200

black Levi 501s. But only because I saw you with them on in Saltcoats a couple of weeks ago. You've actually got quite a cute butt, Joey Burns. And I don't mean cute like Rab Guthrie's.' She studies me. 'But we're gonna have to do something about yer hair.'

'What's wrong with my wig? I style it myself.'

'It's too late to get it cut now. Unless yer mum's got time later on tonight.'

'Eh . . . I go to A Cut Above The Rest, I'll have you know. I've got my club card membership and everything now.' I go over to my desk and open the drawer, fumbling inside to find it. 'It's here somewhere . . .' Only I see something else first and – No! – Sally spots the scrapbook before I get a chance to slip it under some magazines.

'Lemme see it!' Sally's up behind me, pulling the scrapbook out of my hands with a huge grin. 'Yer not saving Melanie Anderson's articles? Yer so *soft*. And I believed ya when you pretended you didn't know Mel was on the school paper!'

'C'mon, Sal. Gimme it back!' I quickly snatch it off her, then put it back, slamming the drawer shut. 'We were talkin' about my wig – not ma woman!'

'Yer wig for your woman, ya mean. Yer gonna need some serious styling for tomorrow night. Wanna borrow my hairdryer and mousse?'

'I've got my own kit, thanks.'

'Then you obviously haven't learned how to

201

use it yet. But don't worry, big brother, 'cause that's why I'm here. I'm gonna show ya how. Right now, as a matter of fact.'

And then Sally starts tugging at my hair in the mirror, slapping my 'haircare' products all over my wig.

'Ow! Must you be so sore?'

'No pain, no gain, pal. Have ya got a deodorant?'

'Whatja mean?' I have a quick sniff in my armpit area. 'There's nothing wrong with me.'

'I mean for tomorrow night, moron. Make sure ya remember to wear it.'

'Any other helpful comments or practical criticisms, coach.'

'Have ya got aftershave?'

''Course I have.'

'Is it a use it or lose it brand?'

'Whatja mean?'

'Am I gonna have to pinch some of my dad's posh aftershave for ya?'

'I've got loads of that myself, actually.'

'OK, then you've passed the physical examination.'

'Ah good, we're finished.' I stand up but Sally pulls me back down by the shirt sleeve. I look at her. 'You *are* leaving, aren't ya?'

'You're too immature for Melanie Anderson.'

'She's in fifth year, the same as me. It's you who's third year.'

'Girls at our age, in case you didn't know it,

are at least two years more mature than boys the same age.'

'Oh, so what yer saying is, Melanie's not really seventeen but nineteen going on twenty.'

'More like going on twenty-five.'

'So, Sally. Instead of being fifteen, you're actually the same age as me now.'

'At least.'

'So yer not just seventeen – but eighteen. I can believe it, actually. The way ya jump in the middle of our mums when they're having a girlie gossip session.'

'Funny ya should say that, 'cause "girls' talk" is next.'

'So talk.'

'OK, y'know it's just going to be you and her alone together. The last thing either of you want are awkward little pauses in the conversation. You'll feel nervous, of course. And so will she, even if she doesn't show it. It's better to talk about anything than suffer that kind of silence. And, Joey, don't recite all the interesting-to-you-only football facts you can remember since Celtic won the European Cup in 1967. Just don't try too hard. Just be yourself.' She studies me again. 'Well, maybe try a little. Only don't put up a false image. Ya won't be able to live up to it later when she finds out what yer really like. The way I know ya.'

'I'm starting to catch on, coach. Oh, I know.' I return her smile. 'A couple of jokes would be good for breaking the ice at first.' I click my fingers and sigh. 'Only thing is, I can never remember any. I could always try and memorise some, huh?'

'Are you joking?'

'I'm trying to help.'

'No, it's *me* who's trying to help.'

'It's OK to say talk about anything. But if I can't break the ice there's going to be a big freeze on the girls' talk.'

'Well, compliment her on her clothes, then. Use yer numb nut, for once! That'll get the chat going when you first meet her. But don't run through an itemised list of what she's got on, going: "Oh hi, Mel. Love yer jacket, jumper, trousers, socks, shoes". Just tell her with an overall sweep, saying simply: "You look nice". Or even: "You look gorgeous". But don't say: "Know something, Mel, you could be a film babe as well". Trust me, Joey, you might think yer giving her a compliment, but she won't like it.'

'Howja know I was gonna say that?' I look at Sally looking at my posters on the wall. I grin. 'She is a birrova babe, though, isn't she?'

'I feel sorry for Melanie Anderson.'

'I thought ya didn't even like her?'

'Oh, I'm older than you, all right. And more mature than I thought.' Sally shakes her head, smiling. 'This is a date heading for disaster.'

My first date with Mel baby!

30

Friday at school. The lunch break. Almost.
12:29 and counting. I can't wait for the bell to
ring so that I can grab a copy of the *School Voice*
and read Melanie's interview and her match
report of the cup final.

Come on.

Come on.

Come on.

Yeees!!!

Running past the other pupils in the corridor, I go racing straight over to the *Voice*
office. I'm so enthusiastic that I even hang
around with Mel for a bit and help her dish out
the paper. There's quite a buzz of activity going
on, I can tell you, with people nipping in and
out non-stop so that I don't really get talking to
Mel that much. Then she asks me to unwrap
more copies from the pile on the floor 'cause
she's run out on the desk. To help meet the
demand, she asks me to set up my own desk on
the other side of the room. It makes sense,
really, when you see the way everybody's
swarming round her desk. Anything for something free, eh? Help yourself, why don'tcha! So

I quickly set up shop with my own news-stand just to help Mel out. She doesn't have to ask me twice.

'I didn't know you had so many readers,' I shout across to her. Well I practically have to shout to get any kind of conversation going with all the noise in here. 'It's a brilliant interview! The whole issue is brilliant!' I really mean it as well. It's not just a put on 'cause my gorgeous love god mug is splashed all over the middle pages. The middle pages! With the title 'Braveheart Burns Wins Us The Cup.'

'Glad you like the feature,' Mel says when the room gets a bit quieter. 'Nice photo, huh?' See what I mean? I don't have to tell you whose bedroom wall the hotshot pin-up is going up on tonight. Tonight! The party. I just can't lose!

'Ya think so?' I feel my face starting to beam. 'Nah, I prefer the one of the team.' I pretend I'm looking at the pic for only the second time now – so she doesn't think I fancy myself. 'It's a good action shot, I suppose. Me running with the ball.'

'I meant the one next to it – of Mr Lovett. I took it myself.'

'I thought old Robin Murray was the school photographer?'

'It wasn't taken at the match. It's in here. The office. Can't you see the noticeboard in the background?'

'So it is . . . Aye, that hunky new TV weatherman has got a twin brother all right.'

'Oh, yes. I see what you mean.' Now Mel's looking at the page with me. Up close and personal, if you see what *I* mean. 'The hair. I've never noticed before.'

'You've given Sally Taylor quite a big bit after all. She's gonna love it when she sees her name there.'

'She's already got some copies. She was here at the morning break.'

I look at Mel, wondering where my special advance copies were.

'Special privilege of staff members, Joey.'

'Really? I thought she would have shown me. She'll probably give me a copy when she gets home.' No! Mel's gonna think I hang around with Sally now. 'She'll probably put it through the letter box when I'm out with my mates down the pool hall. I hardly ever see *wee* Sally, to tellya the truth. At school or at home. Sometimes I forget she even lives near me – never mind, next door. Willya just look at that . . .' I point at the team photo. 'Rab Guthrie's not even looking at the camera. Betcha he's got his eyes on some babe in the crowd. Ya know Rab, eh? Him and his roving eye.'

'I'm still on for tonight,' I tell Mel again, but only when the room is empty. Oh, I'm on, I'm on. Try getting me off, boy. 'If you are, Mel?'

'Of course I am. It's the school party. I wouldn't miss it.'

Then, when I'm still thinking of something cool to say to Mel, old Love it Lovett turns up bang on time again and says, 'I'll take over from you, Joey. You'll miss lunch if you don't hurry.'

I glance over at my girlfriend, hoping she'll be in a hurry to go to the dining hall, too. But she's too busy gazing into Lovett's eyes with that gushy teacher's pet look of hers.

'I would *love* to join you,' Melanie tells me, teasingly. 'But I've got another wee packed lunch with me. And I still haven't finished tidying up in here.'

Well, I wouldn't want to spoil yer fun, darlin'. Naw, you carry on flirting there with my football coach. Don't tell me she's got a crush on him now!

'Go on, boy,' Lovett says. 'Hurry along now.'

Aye, I'm hurrying, I'm hurrying all right. And I'll be hurrying back, too.

To my girlfriend!

'See ya later!'

I head for my 'Lean Cuisine' mince and potatoes in the dining hall, where Rab Guthrie is waiting. Only someone else is waiting for me as well. In the corridor just outside the *School Voice* office. With his rugby scrum standing right behind him. News travels fast.

'Heard you're taking the school prom queen to the party tonight,' Slimey Climie says. 'Must have been some interview you gave our talented reporter, Braveheart. It is Braveheart?'

So Sally was right. Slimey has got it in for me.

'Whadaya want, Climie?'

'Now, is that any way to talk to a fellow sportsman? I only wanted to congratulate you on winning the cup – and the girl. You scored twice, hotshot. In the game, I mean. Good goals. How's your little leg injury, by the way? Painful still, I'll bet.' As if he cared.

'Thanks for the Get Well card.' I give a false smile while I try to stare him out. 'If that's all, I'd like to try and squeeze by your bodyguards.'

'Mellow out, mate.' Slimey thrusts an outstretched arm against the wall, blocking my way. 'I've got no hard feelings about you dating my former girlfriend. Best man wins, eh? I'm all for good sportsmanship, as you know.'

You're not my mate, *mate*, I feel like telling him. Don't think I can't see the bodyguards sniggering away in the background. I'm not showing them I'm scared. I'm not giving them the satisfaction. So I pull my best hardman pose and say nothing.

'See you at the party tonight, then.'

I still don't say anything.

'You are going, Braveheart? They are presenting you with the cup again, y'know.'

'I'll be there.'

'And so will we, won't we, boys?'

'Wouldn't miss it,' say the boys. All together. In unison. In their rugby scrum formation.

'What's going on out there?' Mr Lovett calls through the open classroom door. And then the next minute he's standing there beside us.

'It's OK, *sir*!' Slimey says loudly.

Lovett steps forward. 'That's quite enough of that, William. You've been warned before about your attitude. Don't make me give you detention again.'

'Let's go,' Slimey tells his scrum, who head towards the stairs. Then he looks at me and says, 'See you tonight, Braveheart.'

31

I'm sitting with Rab Guthrie in Luigi's Café down town. Rab's sipping a cappuccino as well and I stare at him over the rim of my coffee cup as I wonder what it is he's got to say, what couldn't wait, what he couldn't tell me at school, what's so important that he had to drag me all the way away from the dining hall and my mince and tatties in the lunch hour.

I've already told him about my little run-in with Slimey Climie and what Sally told me about them planning to drop-kick my head round the rugby pitch after the party (or something). That's all we've spoken about, actually, on the long walk from school. I haven't given Rab the chance to tell me *his* good news yet.

Rab says not to worry 'cause he'll back me up. But I *am* worried. Not so much about Slimey 'cause I reckon I could handle him myself. I'm more worried about his bodyguards 'cause I've seen the rugby players in action. They might have been knocked out of the cup early this season, but they're a team all right. A brat pack of bruisers when they get their weightlifters' arms wrapped round each other's thick necks and shoulders for a scrum and start pushing and shoving and kicking for the ball at their feet (or something else that's rugby ball-shaped). It's enough to give you a sore head just thinking about it.

Anyway, Luigi's Italian Café is the place we usually nip into on Saturday afternoons for a quick cappo when we're hanging out down the shops eyeing up the girls. The caff's got that old time feel that Rab and I like. I mean, it's got modern decor and all that, mixed with all these old-fashioned paintings of famous Italian tourist attractions on the walls – you know, the Leaning Tower of Pizza and that before they built Pizza Huts. Rab says it brings out the old artistic inspiration in him. I only hope it brings out his wallet as well. See, there's also this very up-to-date smell in the air of a fresh coffee aroma mixing with fried sausage and hamburgers, that's making me feel starving! Now that I've missed my mince and tatties and whatever mouth-watering dessert they had laid on at school especially for me. For the meal I've already paid for, I mean. Aye, it's definitely Rab's turn to dig deep today, all right.

The café's an odd place to bring me, all the same, if he wants privacy. It's packed with people . . . shovelling down grub!

Finally, Rab says, 'I just wanted to thank ya. Fur what you've done fur me.'

'Whadaya mean? What've I done?'

212

'Let's get some nosh in first, mate. I'm starving.' He grins. 'Ma treat.'

We order a cheese toastie and a vegetarian mince pie with a double portion of baked beans.

'Wilma Rubber Fingers asked me to stay behind after art class this morning. She said ya had a wee talk with her – aboot me.'

'Oh, Rab! What did she say? Can she do anything for ya?'

'She was a bit surprised at first. Me interested in goin' tae art school and that. As ya know, I'm not exactly everyone's favourite pupil at Millglen Academy.' He starts to grin. 'She thought I wasn't applying myself in class. I told her I didn't know I could. Then she asked me to get ma portfolio together and bring it in fur her.'

'Can she get you in art school?'

'Hang on a minute, let me finish first.' He means the veggie pie. 'So then,' Rab says through a mouthful of beans, 'she starts telling me to bring in this painting and that one and starts running through this list of work I've done in her class. I mean, how can she remember what paintings I've done?'

'She's an art teacher, remember.'

'That's what I mean. She actually remembers ma work. She's no' some drunk punter doon the pub going, "Oh aye, son, that's nice", but not wanting to pay fur ma paintings. Wilma

213

Rubber Fingers is an art teacher. She says I've got talent.'

'Ya must have talent if yer selling them down the pub. Another wee Guthrie sideline?'

'I didn't mean that one to slip oot there. I don't want ya thinkin' I'm fancying myself as some kind of trendy artist noo.'

'I told Wilma ya were into that famous American artist, by the way. Edward Hopkins.'

'It's Hopper. Edward Hopper.'

'Is it? Jeez, I haven't spoiled it for ya?'

'Don't be daft. Why d'ya think yur gettin' the wee cheese toastie treat.' He beams. 'It looks as if things are workin' oot for me after all.'

'Oh, Rab, they will. If Wilma's helping ya.'

'Not only is old Wilma gonna put a word in for me with the rector, she's gonna ring up this teacher mate of hers at Glasgow Art School.'

'The old bible network, eh?'

'The veggie network more like it. Ya told her aboot the slaughterhoose, didn't ya?'

'Sorry, Rab. I couldn't keep my big gob shut. I just got carried away a bit pleading yer case.'

Rab pats his pockets for a second, trying to find a tip for the waitress. 'Hey, and that's not all, boy. Wilma started talkin' aboot all these grants I could get to help pay ma way. So that should keep ma faither happy and hopefully keep me oot of the slaughterhoose.' He gives me one of his leery grins. 'I thought artists had to pay nude models – but they're gonna pay *me*!' He leans forward in his seat. 'Willya

214

promise to keep yer big gob zipped about what we've been talkin' aboot?'

'Not if ya don't want me to.'

'You'll no' spill the beans aboot ma further education plans, willya? 'Cause I'm gonna have to stay on for the exams noo. Well, the Art Higher Grade at least.'

I hold my nose for a laugh. 'As long as *you* promise not to spill the beans till we're out of the café.'

'I've got ma hardman image tae live up tae here,' Rab says, trying hard to stifle a grin, and something else, I'll bet. He shifts uncomfortably in his seat. 'I don't want tae be a soft target for any old nerd at school, y'know.'

'Rab,' I tell him, grinning. 'I wouldn't want ya any other way.'

Then I think of Slimey Climie and another soft target at school and my smile fades. 'We'd better be getting back. We're late enough as it is.'

'Aye.' Rab laughs suddenly. 'Let's get some fresh air.'

Love it Lovett's alone when I get back to the *Voice* office. I'm just about to sneak off when he sees me at the door and waves me in.

'Hi.'

'Hello, sir.' I add, slowly, 'Is Melanie not around, then?'

'You've just missed her, actually. She's just popped off to class.'

215

If there's a look of disappointment on my face, I'm trying hard not to show it. 'I'd better be running off myself.'

'I'm just shutting up shop here, too.' He dumps his briefcase on the desk and starts opening drawers. 'You look a little run down, Joey. Feeling OK? Got over your injury all right?'

'Yes, sir.'

He starts putting things in his briefcase and the bin by the desk.

We'll all miss him in the team. His team.

'Sorry to see you leaving, sir.'

'Thanks, Joey. It's always nice to know that some pupils will miss me.' He smiles. 'I'm sure the majority will be only too glad to see the back of me.'

He probably doesn't know about the little send-off we're giving him tonight. He's been too busy arranging the party and the presentation for *us*. Shows what a top bloke he is really. For a teacher, I mean. And a Chelsea and England supporter.

'Thanks for everything you've done for us, coach. The team was pretty useless till you came along and rescued us.'

'It was, wasn't it.' He smiles again. 'I'm glad you dropped by, actually. I wanted to wish you the very best of luck in your football career. You've got a rare talent there and I know you'll do well. I know I'll be first in the queue at Hampden Park when you play for Scotland.'

He laughs. 'If you give me time to settle in up in Glasgow first, Braveheart.'

'Thanks, sir. See you tonight, then?'

'Tonight.'

32

'Sit still, *willya*.' Sally's holding her hairdryer to my head like a Black & Decker power drill as she bores a hole through my burning brain. And that's not all that's giving me a pain in my red neck right now. She's supposed to be helping me, styling my hair for my hot date with Melanie, while offering words of girlie wisdom and encouragement. But all I can hear is her screaming above the sound of the hairdryer, trying to worm out more details about my snog strategy. Not that I have one, mind. Which explains why I'm squirming on the edge of the stool with my lips zipped.

'C'mon, Sal.' I look at the clock in the kitchen again. 'I'm gonna be late.'

'You've got loads of time. It's not even half five yet.' She slaps me on the back of the head. 'Stop moving, I said. I'll make a mess.'

Girls with hairdryers should have a gun permit to use them – or else have their weapons confiscated by the police.

'Where ya meeting Mel?' Sally shouts in my lughole.

'The car park,' I tell her.

'Across the road from the school?'

'I know where it is, thank you.'

'That's where William Climie parks his BMW.'

'Melanie isn't going in *his* car, geek. She's going with me. That's why yer giving me the love god make-over, remember?'

'Well, you can't drive . . . so whose car is she going in, then?'

'Her dad's dropping her off, as a matter of fact.'

'Not a good sign, Joey.'

'Whadaya mean?'

'Well, what other vet do you know'll be waiting outside in a Range Rover half an hour before the party ends.'

'He's only making sure she gets home all right.'

'Not a good sign, Joey.'

Do you think *I* don't know that!

'How ya gonna link lips with Mel if the vet's on call?'

'We'll probably have a smooch during one of the slow songs.'

'Ya still don't have a clue, do you?' Sally switches the hairdryer off but her voice is still loud. 'Ya mean yer gonna get it on with her *there*? In the crowded assembly hall with everybody watching?'

'Lower the decibels, DJ. I'm not at the party yet. My maw's in the other room.'

'Have you thought this through, Joey?'

219

Well maybe not.

'Well, what should I do?' I ask her.

I hate the sound of my sad lad voice sometimes.

'Apart from don't go, Joey, I don't know what else to tell you.'

'A big help you are, coach.'

Sally grabs me by the scruff, creasing the CK 'tee' she spent half an hour ironing. 'I've done yer hair, told ya what togs to wear, *tried* to give ya some girlie advice. But I'm sorry, Joey. There's nothing else I can do for you now. You're on yer own!'

'Sal—'

'I'm outta here.'

And then Sally's at the door.

And I'm just behind her.

Girls!

'Don't go yet,' I say, hoping she'll stay. Until I'm ready to go out, I mean.

'Morag'll be here soon. I told you she was coming round tonight.'

'Look, Sal.' She turns to face me. 'Thanks for all your help. I really mean it.' I smile. 'See ya later.'

'Oh, you'll see me all right.' She steps outside, grinning. 'And sooner than ya think.'

I knew it! She'd better not be here when I get back. Waiting with her reporter's notebook for a big love match exclusive.

'Just be careful, Joey, that's all. I'm worried

about William Climie. What he might do to you.'

Oh, that's what it is.

'I can handle Slimey,' I call out. It's my other date I'm more worried about.

Sally blows me a kiss goodbye at the gate.

'Good luck with yer hot date, Babeheart!'

Then she runs away giggling to her girlie night in.

I wish she was going now, as well. I'm going to need all the luck I can get!

33

Friday night is *paaaarty nite*!

I'm on time. I'm not late. So where's my date? What's keeping ya, Mel baby! I was five minutes early for the seven-thirty kick-off time, you know. OK, ten minutes. OK, twenty. But that was half an hour ago! I'm still standing alone at the car park across the road from the school, watching everybody else walking into the blare of happ'nin' music I can hear even here. They never told us it was going to be a golden oldies night. Don't tell me the bloke with headphones spinning the decks is MC Bates the headmaster blaster? Next thing you know, Rab's fave hippy chick Wilma Rubber Fingers'll be getting her Heavy Metal axe out for an air guitar headbangin' sesh! At least the music's loud, I suppose, and the 'disco lights' are bound to be flashing more than the Christmas tree they usually prop up in the assembly hall. Oh, well, party on dude, eh?

Just as I'm looking at my watch again I spot this big green 'n' creme Range Rover bombing along the road in second gear and I see Melanie sitting in the front seat next to her dad. Even from here I can tell that the old vet is going to be his usual cheerful and charming whenever-you-see-him-in-Safeways self as he sits hunched up over the steering wheel, peering through the windscreen for somewhere to park.

No! What large cuddly creature is that taking up all three back seats in the vet's luxuriously spacious Range Rover. Well, it's not Mel's mum. And she doesn't have a BIG sister. So it must be her best mate, Lucy Harper.

This is not happening to me!

I walk down the street to meet them, gazing away from the glare that isn't coming from the car headlights. Aye, that's right, Mr Anderson. It's me. I'm the boyfriend.

The passenger doors open slowly and a scent of posh perfume wafts tantalisingly towards me as Melanie's elegantly sandaled feet step gracefully out – followed by that big beach ball and chain for the evening bouncing right out after her. Is that *really* pink trousers and a green and orange T-shirt Lucy Harper's got on? Oh, I know, I should be kind, not cruel. We don't get that many school parties after all, and Juicy Lucy'll probably never get the chance to wear her Cinderella gown again. This is *my* hot date, not hers! Well, I'm sorry, Lucy, luv . . . but you're not spoiling my BIG night out!

I've only got eyes for Mel. My gorgeous girlfriend looks stunning in that slinky little black slip dress that reveals lo-o-o-o-o-ng cheerleader legs. And as she slips back in the car for a second to grab her tiny cashmere cardigan, I notice that her dad is proud of his daughter's natural beauty, too. Looks, I might add, that she obviously gets from her mum 'cause fat, stumpy, baldy little vets with loadsa money usually marry ex-models, don't they? So the papers are always saying anyway. Well, Mr Friendly just gave me the old silent warning nod of recognition, didn't he? Dads don't like me, for some reason. Dads with daughters, I mean. Not just detective dads – vet dads, too. I don't really know any more dads with daughters. And I don't really want to. Don't they remember when they were my age? When they were – Weh hey! – one of the lads!

'Enjoy yourselves, girls,' he says, waving through the slowly closing electric window as the car pulls out from the kerb.

Oi, vet! I'm going to the party as well, y'know!

'You've got the mobile, Melanie, phone me and let me know how you're getting back home or if you want me to pick you up.'

A subtle little *double reminder* there in case I'm planning any party tricks of my own after-wards or hoping to cadge a lift home in the comfortably *un*-spacious vetmobile with Mel and Juicy Lucy.

'Do you and Lucy know each other?' Melanie asks, uncomfortably.

'Only from a distance,' I say, thinking: Aye, as far away as possible, pal!

We swap smiles, and mine is really false.

'I feel I know you already, Lucy. I'm sure we'll be lovey-dovey mates before the night is over.'

They both give me funny looks.

So why am *I* not laughing?

The 'girls' walk together, and I tag along behind 'cause Lucy Harper won't (or can't, more like it!) shift over a teeny, weeny bit for three abreast. I'm not even listening to their boring *girlie* gossip . . . I didn't know Nathan Hodge was snogging Clare Ralston? And Kelly Bruce is going out with wee Pat Duncan! Wait till I tell Rab Guthrie!

We're through the school gate and then outside the building and I still haven't got a word in. Strobe lights flicker behind the black air-raid curtains covering the assembly hall windows. Pulsating music pounds through the thick brick prison walls. At least things are looking up in the music department. The hardmen posse must be filling in while the DJ has a quick break in the ambulance speeding to the casualty ward at Lawson Hospital.

And then we're in the building and walking along the corridor towards the deafening we'll-have-to-shout-to-speak-in-a-minute   music. Thanks for sharing that with me, Mel. But on ya go – don't mind me, darlin' – carry on chatting away with Juicy Lucy. Obviously there are no teachers near the volume control as the hardmen turn the 'sounds' up to the max. Not that I'm getting the chance to speak or shout much as we enter the decorated assembly hall 'pleasure dome'.

34

'Oh, I *love* that single – don't you, Joey?'

'Yeah, love it, Mel.'

And talking about our former football coach, who is standing over by the stage chatting to some of the lads in the team. 'Y'know why old Lovett's in such a hurry to get back to Glasgow, don'tcha?'

Mel quickly looks away from him as I whisper to her, 'He's got a babe. She goes to college there as well.'

'*How d'you know?*'

I've got her attention now, all right! Can't wait to tell Juicy Lucy some more hot girlie gossip when she gets back from the refreshment room, eh?

'He was spotted with her in his babemobile.'

'It's a car, Joey. And I wish you'd stop using those dreadful sayings. You're so immature sometimes.'

What sayings? Me, immature?

You're too immature for Melanie Anderson.

'Eh, I'll be gettin' a set of wheels as well, Mel, when I pass my driving test. Did I tellya I was taking lessons soon?' Letting her know –

maturely, manly, of course – that romantic drives in the country are high on the agenda with me next summer; when I'm old enough to drive, I mean.

Mel looks surprised. 'D'you know what Mr Lovett's girlfriend looks like?'

'Gorgeous, of course, like *you* . . .' I give her one of my wee flirty smiles but she doesn't seem too flattered with the compliment. 'Well, old Lovett is quite good looking, I suppose. He's bound to have pulled a stunner.'

'Maybe he has a sister.'

'Aye, that's what Rab said as well. But this bird was pure blonde apparently. And you know' – I nod over at Lovett – 'how dark his hair is.'

'So you don't really know anything about this girl.'

'Well, I, er . . . no, not really.'

'Well you can't just jump to conclusions about other people. That's how you get into trouble. You'd better watch Mr Lovett doesn't find out you're spreading rumours about him.'

'I haven't told anyone yet.' Not even Sally. What's Mel getting all worked up about! 'You're the first to know.'

'Well maybe you should try and keep it that way.'

Now we're standing side by side at the edge of the dance floor like a happily married couple . . . as if the polite conversation Mel and

228

I are sharing is for appearances' sake only, I mean. It's weird when you're with a girl like Melanie Anderson who you're crazy about. Although I can't keep my eyes off her it's as if she's not there – or more like I'm not there, the way she seems to be avoiding physical contact with me.

Then a slow song comes on. How romantic, eh? Yeah *right*. The only intimate moment we've shared so far was when our arms touched fleetingly when we stood to the side to let Lucy Harper make room for some skinny little kid to squeeze past her in the corridor. That was an awkward moment all right. Up close and personal with Mel – and didn't she know it, boy. The way she seemed to tense at my touch.

Juicy Lucy's gone to the laydeez' room, by the way. And you'd think Mel was way across the other side of the dance floor the way we're hardly looking at each other never mind trying to shout above the music. That dry-ice drifting up through the air should be cocooning us in a clinch as we smooch our way around the dance floor and . . .

'That tear gas is chokin' me, Climie. You've let too much out again. Somebody open the fire exit!'

Thanks for that quick reality check there. Glad the rugby scrum are having a fun night out – 'cause I know I'm not.

Lucy Harper's actually all right. Once you get

229

past the dazzling wardrobe clash, I mean. Her chat is way cooler than her clothes. She's a blast. A really good laugh. Which is good for me, in a way, 'cause Mel keeps disappearing all the time. 'Sorry, Joey, but I've got some quick backstage arrangements to do for the cup presentation later', or, 'Be back in a minute, Joey, I just have to pop up to the *Voice* office to pick up the surprise going-away present for Mr Lovett.'

That one was twenty minutes ago. She must be gift-wrapping the pressie with gold paper and ribbons, the time it's taking her. Aye, and leaving me alone again with the consolation prize. Oh, I shouldn't take it out on Lucy.

To be honest, I'm feeling a bit guilty over the way I acted with her when the girls first arrived. She must have felt the same way I did when Melanie's dad gave me the big cold shoulder treatment. I was a real jerk. I admit it. So to show there's no hard feelings on my part – and that I actually quite like her company in the absence of my proper girlfriend – I'm making it up to the 'party girl' (and boy is *she* wild!) by giving her a couple of quick twirls round the dance floor.

Go on . . . rattle yer pocket, Joey! That's right, I even splash out on Juicy Lucy at the refreshment room and buy her a can of Diet Pepsi. She asked for it, by the way, after I offered to buy her whatever *she* wanted. Well there's only Diet Pepsi and Irn-Bru and Vimto. She's an all right gal, after all, my new mate,

230

Lucy. Only she's not there when I get back. She's disappeared on me as well! Are the girls trying to tell me something?

Rab Guthrie comes over with a big grin on his face and gives me a quick glimpse of the cider bottle poking out of the inside pocket of his baseball jacket.

'Gotta go, Joey, the chicks are waiting.'

Ben Robinson comes over to gate-crash the private party, his arm round his best mate for the night. 'Y'know the good thing about getting sozzled?' he tells Rab as they turn to leave. 'Even the ugly birds can get a snog!'

I spot Slimey Climie again, eyeing me from the other side of the dance floor. He comes over. 'Would buy you a beer, mate, but they only sell soft drinks at school parties.' So he gives me one of his sneering smiles instead. 'Just wanted you to know that if you and your girlfriend are looking for a lift later, I'll be outside in the car park waiting.'

'You're a great guy, William,' I say icily.

'See you later, then. Ciao!'

'Enjoying yourself?' Melanie asks as she slips into the empty seat next to me.

'I am now.' I squeeze her hand. 'Wanna dance?'

I can tell Mel's suitably impressed with my dazzling moves the way we're burning up the dance floor here. She wraps her arms round my neck for a second and throws her head back with laughter.

'Not dancing, sir?' she calls out as Mr Lovett walks past.

But her small voice gets lost in the noise and he doesn't hear her, so I say, 'This dance is already taken, darlin' . . .'

Just for a laugh, like.

It's not my fault Mel doesn't have a sense of humour!

And when we come straight off after the song finishes without staying on for the next slushy body blender, Mel says, 'Just because we arrived together, doesn't mean we have to stay together.' She gestures toward the crowd in the corner. 'Go and have a chat with your mates if you're bored.'

Which is pure tosh, 'cause I've been talking to everybody all night and not just Lucy Harper.

'Fancy going to the flicks tomorrow night?' I ask Mel during another lull in the *non*-lurve talk. Well I had to say something.

'What?'

'Yer supposed to say *when*.' I slip my arms round Mel, but I feel her stiffen at my touch again. 'For our next date, *girlfriend*. We can go to the flicks tomorrow night if ya like. Whatja say, eh?'

'I don't know. I'll have to wait and see what I've got planned first.'

232

I can hear my sad lad's voice saying, 'Wanna rent some videos one night this week? Monday, Tuesday, Wednesday, Thursday ... Friday, even. I'm easy.'

Bet Mel isn't.

'I wish you'd stop rushing things, Joey. Let's just wait and see.'

I'm not rushing. I can wait.

'Saturday's OK as well, Mel. As long as we don't miss *Sportscene: Match of the Day.*'

'Now we wouldn't want to miss that, would we?' she says as she slowly shakes her head. And then goes to look for Lucy.

See, I knew she was a secret football fan!

I slip among the crowd of people spilling out into the corridor for a breather from the hot, sweaty assembly hall 'atmosphere'. All the cola-sippers and the just-pulled couples dying for a snog if only the overhead lights weren't so bright. Don't they know that's why they *are* so bright!

I look around for Melanie but she's nowhere in sight. Then, through a break in the crowd, I see the main door opening at the far end of the corridor and a girl, who I can't quite recognise from here, hurrying in alone. A cloud of dry-ice seems to seep through from the dance floor as the DJ spins a sexy saxophone song, as if on cue. But I'm not listening – I'm looking! Who's the new girl at school? I want to know. I'm practically straining my neck here to get a better

233

look without trying to appear too sensual/ obvious/desperate. And still she rushes eagerly towards me, her bag swinging from her shoulder and her long reddish-brown hair swirling brightly around her. Towards me! This chick is doing the trick for me all right in those vaguely familiar tomboy togs . . . Levi jacket, jeans, trainers. Come to me mystery girl as I . . . snap out of the fantasy!

'*What are you doing here, Sally?*'

'Told ya you'd see me later.'

'Another hint of a tint?' I say, totally blown away.

'Ya like it?'

'You'll never get in. This is a fifth and sixth year party.'

'Don't I look like sixth year tonight?'

'C'mon, Sal. What'ya doing here?'

And then she bursts out laughing.

'Yer girlfriend's been pulling rank again.' Sally flashes the yellow Press Pass badge she's got pinned on the tight white tee underneath her jacket. 'She got me the hot ticket.'

'For the party?'

'I'm after a scoop, pal! I'm covering the cup presentation for the school paper.' Sally opens her kitbag, showing me her journo's tool kit: camera, Dictaphone, notebook, pens. 'Melanie and Mr Lovett are too busy with the presentation. So which other cub reporter with her first byline do you know who can hack it?' She grins. 'And ya know I love trouble!'

234

'Oh you're Taylor-made for trouble, all right. You *knew* you'd be here all along. When you were' – I look around, lowering my voice – 'styling my wig for me. If I knew that you—'

'You're here at last, Sally,' a voice calls out. A Chelsea supporter's voice. And then Mr Lovett and Melanie are standing beside us, looking all hot and flustered.

'We're just about to do the cup presentation,' Mel says excitedly. 'Are you two ready?'

'Oh, I'm ready all right,' Sally says, staring at me with that mischievous look in her eyes that can only mean trouble.

35

They're cranking the amps up again and the strobe lights are flashing away. We've had the presentations on the stage – the 'Well done!' one for us, and the 'Goodbye, good luck!' one for Mr Lovett. Old Robin Murray, the school snapper, even had the camera out for another team shot and we got to hold the cup all over again for the cheering crowd on the dance floor. Now we're partying on to the old sing-a-long football anthem favourite:

'*We are the champions . . . We are the champions . . . tra, la, la . . .*'

I've got my eyes on Sally. I've got them on her, and I can't keep them off her. You should see the way she's rushing all over the place with that notebook and pen of hers, grabbing quick quotes from all the players for a follow-up feature on our victorious team for the next issue of the *School Voice*. I stand there like a big brother, proudly watching her blagging away with all the other lads. The other lads? *Lads*? I'm getting a bit jealous and possessive here, to tell you the truth. Now I know why some of my mates were clamming up on me when I was quizzing them about their sisters. I'll be keeping an eye on old Sally tonight, all right, 'cause I know all about these *lads*.

'Doesn't Sally look lovely?' Mel says, smiling at me.

'Aye . . .' I tell her. 'We're best mates, y'know.'

Then the dancing starts up and Mel asks to be 'excused' again. She nips off to the laydeez' make-over station, this time to powder her nose or whatever else it is they do in there when they're making themselves irresistible for us. Still no sign of Lucy Harper. Maybe she's powdering her nose as well? I'd love to know what girls do in the bogs? When they're having girlie chats and that, I mean. I wonder what girls gab about. Probably about some poxy new lipstick they're all giving the road test on their kissers before they come out and smear it all over some boring little ugly nerd's collar – like Jimmy Cairns over there! So why's Mel not smearing me with her posh L'Oreal lipstick!

I've got a red lipstick neck now. I feel more like that ex-boyfriend of Melanie's standing over there and giving me the evil eye. Go and dance with yerself, gorgeous! Get outta my face, Slimey, willya! Everybody knows I'm here with Mel – so why isn't *Mel* here with *me*? Even Sally's noticed I'm on my own again.

Five minutes later, the only cub reporter with her first byline who I *know* is heading for trouble with *this* team player, manages to catch me in a dark corner alone. She laughs. 'I fooled ya about Morag coming round, huh? Why d'ya think I was in such a hurry after I did your wig for you?'

'Listen, Cub . . .' I pretend I'm shouting in Sally's ear because of the music, but really it's because I could kill her. 'The first rule of journalism is that a reporter never reveals her source. I did my own wig – d'ya get me?'

'I get you, I get you . . . *Babeheart*.'

'Yer new wig looks nice, by the way. It's not often ya get a compliment from me.'

Sally gives me a funny look. 'You're not the only boy who's been flirting with me tonight, Joey Burns. I've been giving the lads the hint with my tint, all right. Yer not the only boy who's got my home phone number now.'

'You've not been giving yer number out to that bunch of beauties? Do they know yer dad's got the phone bugged; that he carries handcuffs even when he goes on holiday.'

'My business card, moron.' Sally slips me one; white with black type. 'Ya like them? My dad got them done for me at the cop shop. All very official looking.' She smiles. 'I'm starting up as a freelancer for any teen mag that'll let me interview football totty.' She shoves her notebook in my face. 'Now it's your turn.'

'Haven't ya forgotten something?' I say, without even thinking. 'Ya should have waited till ya moved to Dumfries first.' I quickly add,

'Now yer gonna have to get new cards printed before you try and pull any more footballer boyfriends down there.'

Sally blushes slightly. 'Aye, well I haven't left yet. And know what?' She turns to leave, 'The slow songs are coming on now . . .'

With the slow songs starting and Melanie gone again, all I can do is stand on the touch-line and watch Sally slip into the arms of . . . *me*.

'Ya haven't asked me to dance yet, Joey?'

''Cause you've been too busy chatting up all my mates, that's why.'

Aye and they all fancy her, too, if you ask me. I quickly grab her hand, letting the lads know that this dance is already taken. That wee wind-up merchant! She almost had me fooled again! I actually thought she was up for a slow song shuffle there with one of the lads.

We stay up for two dances and then Sally says, 'I'd better go.'

'You're always saying—'

'But I'll be back for another dance.'

She's smiling, and so am I.

'I've still got some of yer football team to talk to.'

'I'll be waiting on ya,' I say, wondering where this is leading and who's leading who on.

'I won't be long, Joey.'

'Have ya seen Mel?' I ask Rab, casually, when

239

he comes in the hall. 'She was, erm, getting me another Pepsi, I think.'

'I just left her in the corridor there with old Lovett,' he says, grinning. 'She was helping him carry that very heavy paperweight and posh pen, that the teachers gave him fur his going-away pressie, tae his car.'

I grin back at him. 'Suppose the pet wants to say a more personal goodbye to her favourite student teacher.' After all, old Lovett's not only shooting off early but leaving the school for good. It's understandable, really, when they've worked so closely together on the paper over the last few months. I'm making excuses for my girlfriend even if she's not making any to me for beating it on me again.

'Aye, I know what ya mean, Joey boy. I was just sayin' ma goodbyes tae the coach, tae.'

Later, that wee roving reporter who's never short of a question or two, slumps down on the seat beside me for a quick breather from the boys. Aye, and don't think I haven't been watching who she's 'interviewing'.

'Ya off duty now?' I say, hoping she'll stay.

Sally sips her cola and sighs, 'That's the kind of lame question I usually ask ma dad.'

'Oh,' I say suddenly, 'have ya asked Sarge yet if he can get me one of those Detective Dictaphones? Before he beats it to Dumfries.'

There, that brings up the subject discreetly. I know Sally's been avoiding it. She hasn't said anything else about Sarge leaving. I mean *her* leaving. I don't want her to go.

'If that's all you want from me, Burnsie, then I'm beating it as well.'

She gets up to go. This time I ask her to stay.

We watch the others dancing while we sit together talking. Well, I'm talking. Sally's listening. She's a good listener. I can really talk to Sally sometimes. Only thing is, I've been getting heavy on her for the last half hour now and I know I'm starting to cringe her a little. That's why I'm whispering – well I have to – in case anyone's tuning in over the music. I don't think they can hear us anyway, not with the deafening 'wall of sound' that surrounds us. Which is good, in a way, 'cause I really need some of Sally's expert girlie advice *now.*

I'm starting to have serious doubts about Melanie Anderson, you know. I don't think she fancies me the way I fancy her. And, to be honest, I don't even think I have the hots for her any more! I mean she's gorgeous, don't get me wrong. But there doesn't seem to be anything there between us. No connection. None of that fatal attraction *reaction* you get in the movies all the time.

Maybe I'm expecting too much from Melanie? Aye, that's probably the reason. After all, it's only the first date. And it is a crowded situation where everybody knows us. I should be chuffed that everyone is clambering all over her because they like her so much. I knew what

I was getting into when I pulled the most popular girl at school. And I knew there was bound to be a downside or two with dating her, too. It goes with the territory, Joey boy. Hotshot – or not!

And then I start telling Sally about my dad. Oh, I have to tell someone! All these crazy, mixed-up feelings I've kept bottled up inside me since my dad died are finally coming to the surface in a mad rush of emotions. I can't stop it. I can't. I think I've finally reached the point where I have to come to terms with things.

As I rewind my mind over the last six weeks since my dad died – no, seven weeks now – I start telling Sally everything. I'm telling her so much until it hurts and I just can't stop myself any more. It sort of comes gushing out of me like I've never wanted to tell anyone anything before. I keep talking and talking until I can't stop.

'I know it hurts,' Sally's saying, 'but you'll get over it. Trust me, you will. It'll take time. Nobody knows what's going to happen in the future. You just have to get on with your life, take it one day at a time, do the best you can.'

Now it's Sally who's doing all the talking and I can't stop her. And I don't even want to stop her . . .

'Soon you'll be playing for Ardrossan Rovers,' she's saying softly. 'I'll even letcha join Kilmarnock when ya turn professional. Ayr

242

United have got enough good players. It's only fair that Killie should have one . . .'

I can feel Sally trembling. Then, all of a sudden, she sits up straight again, slipping her hand away from mine.

'What'ya laughing at, Joey?' And I see that Sally's laughing, too.

'Ya sure this exclusive interview's off the record, Cub?'

'Aye, and yer still a big girl's blouse. Quote me on that: *soft lad*.'

Near the end of the night, Sally gets her notebook and pen out again as she moves in on my other favourite goalkeeper, Rab Guthrie. He's not going to be a happy chappy missing out on the slow songs with all the babes. Hang on a minute? Most of the 'chicks' are up on the floor dancing or are getting ready to go home . . . either with their girlfriends or other guys!

Hey, girls! He's still here! The stud-u-like is standing over there dateless!

Wait till I see that BIG MOUTH later. Sally must still have some players to interview. Hey, she hasn't interviewed *me* yet? Saving the best for last, eh? Waiting for the last dance more like it!

I wish the last dance would last all night . . .

I shut my eyes, swaying gently with the music. Sally's holding me, warm and comforting, my chest getting tighter, heart

243

hammering, until I'm not even trying to cover up holding back what I'm feeling inside.

'No more talk about dying,' she murmurs against my ear, stroking my hair gently. 'You've got everything to live for. You'll play for Scotland one day soon, Joey Burns. And I'll be in the crowd with the rest of the Tartan Army to watch ya, to cheer ya on. Me and yer maw and Rab Guthrie. You've got Laddie to look after now, remember. People care about *you*, Joey. Your mum. *Me*. We love you . . .'

Hazily, I can hear the music, but it's as if I'm standing outside myself, taking part in a crazy dream where everything's happening in slow motion.

Through glazed eyes, I gaze at Sally's face smiling back at me. I suddenly feel light-headed, as if a great weight has been lifted from my shoulders. I feel so different when I'm with her; so relaxed, so at ease compared to how I was with Melanie Anderson.

I tilt Sally's face up to mine and carefully, very softly, flick the hair from her forehead, her wet eyes sparking back at me.

Looking at Sally now, my mind on a future that's not mine to know, I realise that I couldn't bear it if I never saw her again. I've never really thought about what's ahead of us before. For somehow, without even realising it, you take people for granted; get so used to seeing them day-in, day-out that you sort of expect them always to be there for you.

As Sally snuggles closer to me, enveloping me in a sweet, sweet longing for life, to be loved, I find myself lowering my face to hers . . .

I suddenly pull back from kissing Sally as she looks up at me, confusion in her eyes.

What am I doing? I came here tonight with Melanie! She's my girlfriend, not Sally. This is crazy!

I hold Sally awkwardly, clumsily, without speaking, wondering who's watching us, what Sally must be thinking of me, what the hell I thought I was doing!

I move rigidly with the music, wishing the song would end soon. I'm clinging to Sally with my eyes closed tightly, cringing inside, shutting out everything but the music and the music . . .

It's not until the last dance ends rather abruptly and the lights come on suddenly that I find out why Melanie Anderson has been avoiding me all night. Why I thought she'd gone home already. Why she suddenly comes bursting into the hall with a wild desperate look on her face, tries to smooth out her dishevelled party dress as she half-walks, half-runs self-consciously across the dance floor towards me with everybody in the room looking hard at us.

She grabs me by the arm, pulling me away from Sally, panic on her face. I go with Melanie, glancing back at Sally. There's this hurt look in Sally's eyes as if she's just been dumped. And still Melanie's dragging me away with her.

'Oh, my God! I don't know what to do,' Melanie whispers anxiously as we scurry along the corridor. 'I think William Climie's gone crazy! He's with all his gang!'

'So you saw them waiting for me,' I say when we get outside into the dark empty playground. 'Feeling guilty about sneaking off with Lucy?'

Melanie stops suddenly. 'It's not *you* they're after! It's Tristan, I mean Mr Lovett!' She starts running again. 'C'mon, Joey. They've got him cornered in the car park. Hurry!'

We race across the road.

'I thought Mr Lovett left early?' I call out.

'He did. Oh, Joey, I'm sorry . . .' Her sudden deep gasp makes me glance over at her. 'He left with me.'

'*You*?' I say slowly. 'You and Mr Lovett?'

'Climie and his cronies caught us coming out of Tristan's car . . .' She looks at me despairingly. 'I know it was crazy . . . in the car park. We were only having a wee smooch.'

'Mel—'

'There's no time to talk. Hurry!'

36

'Leave him alone, Climie!'

Slimey turns away from Mr Lovett, his hands still pinning the trembling student teacher against the bonnet of his white MG sports car, the rugby scrum surrounding them.

'Butt out, Burns. This has nothing to do with you now. Just be thankful we found out who the tart's real boyfriend is. She's been two-timing you as well!'

'It's easy to act the tough guy,' I tell him, 'when you've got your team backing you up.'

'Think about your own sporting career, hotshot,' Slimey warns me. 'Walk away now, while you can still walk.'

'Take me on my own and leave Mr Lovett alone, ya big jerk.'

Slimey laughs. 'Sod off, Burns. Stop wasting my time, ya wee weed. Can't you see I'm in a hurry to get to the pub before it closes.'

It is quite funny when you think about it, 'cause I'm a really crap fighter. I've only been in two fights, both at primary school, and I got beat both times. I don't know what came over me there for a second. I wasn't even thinking about my own safety. Now everybody's looking at me, not only Melanie. All I know is that if Slimey won't fight me fairly, I'm going to have to jump in for Mr Lovett and get wasted as well. I'm not trying to act tough or show off in front of Mel. It's too late for that. I would try and help anyone in trouble, if I could. I really would. Even a guy who's just stolen my girl-friend. Even though I know now that she never really was.

'Me and you, Climie, in an even fight,' I say. 'Just let Mr Lovett go.'

'Now it's you who's being very foolish, Joey,' Mr Lovett says, trying to struggle free. Slimey clamps him harder against the car bonnet with a loud metallic thud.

'Shut it, you English sod,' Slimey says, losing his temper.

I count seven in the scrum, not including Slimey. Not looking good, Joey . . .

Melanie stammers, 'Someone's bound to have called the police by now. I think we should all just forget what's happened and go home.'

If someone had called the cops they would have been here by now. I live next door to a rozzer, remember. Trust me, they'd be here.

'I'm staying, Slimey,' I say. 'You're going to have to take me, too.'

Finally, Slimey loses his patience. 'If you want a fight, Burns, the boys will be more than happy to accommodate you. Waste him as well . . .'

The grinning rugby scrum move in on me for the drop-kick. I'm really trembling now but trying hard not to show it. Obviously I still haven't perfected my tough guy pose 'cause the scrum are grinning even more as they close in for the kill. I'm still standing my ground, though, but that's only because I've got nowhere to run.

'Get on with it,' Slimey snarls. 'Kick his poxy face in!'

'Leave him alone!' a girl's voice screams, followed by the clump of fast-approaching footsteps and then Sally's in the car park with us. Her frightened face looks deathly white in the dim streetlights. What's she doing here? Oh God, they'd better not touch her as well!

'Ya'd better do as the lassie says,' Rab Guthrie shouts, running in behind Sally, fighting for breath. Not even his Uzi sub-machine gun trick can back us up now. Sally was right. Rab doesn't stand a chance either.

'Get them, boys.' Climie swings his arm, ready to smack Mr Lovett. 'Waste them all. Waste them!'

Then the football team arrives.

'I got as many of the lads together as I could, Rab,' grins Ben Robinson, giving me a quick thumbs up sign.

'C'mon, boys, waste them!' Slimey's becoming hysterical now, as he begins to lose his nerve. We might wind-up teachers but we would never beat them up. There are some school rules that can never be broken. And Slimey Climie is well out of order tonight.

The rugby scrum versus half the football team. It's an even fight – seven-a-side – but we're still no match for the big hairy bruisers. *Jeez*, and Sally and Melanie are right in the thick of the action!

'C'mon, girls,' I tell them. 'Go on . . . *Run*!'

'I'm no' running any more,' another voice says breathlessly. 'I've just got here. *Whoof* . . . that's ma exercise for the week.'

We all spin round to see Lucy Harper standing there, flexing her pecs with the heavy paperweight present Mr Lovett must have dropped when the scrum jumped him. 'Look what I've found,' she chuckles. 'A concealed weapon.'

Big Ronnie Cowan steps out from behind Lucy.

'Ma bird's got more guts than all you scrum bags,' growls our muscleman captain. 'So don't mess with our team.'

Lucy goes all shy for a second, but I know she's not shy. So that's where my new gal pal's been hiding . . . on the pull!

Her boyfriend winks over at Sally. 'Aye, you're another bird with guts.'

Slimeball knows he's beaten now. He shoves Mr Lovett away harshly, laughing with his scrum as the student slumps to the ground.

Mr Lovett gets to his feet shakily. 'That was a very stupid thing to do, William.' He dusts himself off, his composure returning slowly. 'You haven't left school yet.'

'But you have, *teacher*. You've got no authority here any more,' Slimey tells him, then turns to leave. 'Let's go to the pub, boys.'

'Neither have you, Slimey,' I say, raising my arm to hold the football team back. 'And all these people here are a witness. Don't even think of telling any tales out of school about Mr Lovett and Melanie.'

'And that goes for all you scrum scum,' Lucy Harper says, her arm round her boyfriend. 'Think I don't know ya call me Mrs Michelin, eh? Just remember, boys . . . Big Ronnie and me outweigh the lot of ya.'

What a secret Sumo wrestler! Worra gal!

37

Melanie's on the mobile phone, telling the vet that Lucy's dad will take her home later in his car. Everyone else has left now. The school is closed, the car park empty. Rab and Sally tried to drag me away with them, but I had to stay and settle something that's best said alone with the two love birds.

Lovett's standing just out of talking distance, trying to fix the dent mark Slimey left on the bonnet of his sports car. I watch Melanie pull a face as she listens to her dad moaning away because she didn't phone him earlier. I'm glad she's making the call 'cause I'm struggling to keep my cool as I gaze away from her eyes again.

Jeez, is this the kind of face she was pulling when Lovett and her were laughing behind my back? Oh, here he comes again, the lovesick lad. Quick, pretend you don't see him. What a plonker I must have looked! I'm a laughing stock now. Wait till everybody in my class hears about this on Monday, when the gossip really gets going. They all saw me arriving with Melanie Anderson – and running out of the hall with her. God, I can never show my face at school again! A rage surges through me. My heart is hammering, my stomach churning. I feel sick. 'How could you have done this to me?' I ask her, my voice trembling, as she comes off the phone. 'You knew how I felt about you.'

'I never wanted it to happen this way.'

'*So what way did you, then*?' Anger erupts, filling me with hatred for her. But she's not worth it. I can do better than her.

'Joey . . .' She reaches for my hand. 'Please, let me explain.'

'Don't!' I jerk my arm free. 'Don't even touch me.'

I can't even look at her now, but I want to. What did I do wrong? Confusion swamps me, clouding my thoughts. I want an explanation 'cause I still don't understand what's happening. I just don't know what to think any more.

'Joey,' she says, trying to keep her voice low so loverboy won't hear her. 'I know how you must feel.'

'No you don't,' I say, more quietly this time. 'You've got no idea. You used me.'

'The last thing we wanted was to hurt you.'

We wanted.

In each other's arms.

In his cosy two-seater sports car.

We were only having a wee smooch.

'Are you going to tell me that it suddenly

just happened tonight? When you were saying goodbye to him in his car?'

'No, I'm not going to lie to you.'

My voice rises till I'm almost shouting. 'But you've been lying all this time! How long has it really been going on between you two?'

'Not that long.'

'*How long*?'

'Don't shout, please. I'm trying to explain.'

It suddenly hits me. 'It was you in Lovett's car all this time. That's why Slimey was tearing into you in the playground last week. You were two-timing him as well, weren't you?'

'I've never—'

'Never what? Go on, say it. You've never gone behind another guy's back before.'

'I told William Climie that I didn't want to go out with him again. That's when he started getting rough. He knew there was someone else. He must have thought it was you. He didn't know about Tristan and me until tonight.'

Tristan and me.

Tristan and me.

'That's what I don't get, Mel. Why did you go out with me, if you were already seeing him?'

Him with the car.

Him with my girl.

'I – I'd better be going,' I say, brushing past her, breathing heavily. I feel crushed, cheated. I'm not staying for the rest of her sad sorry story. I've made a big enough mistake staying

254

this long! I'm getting all shaky now and she can see me trembling. I'm still acting like a plonker!

'Joey . . .' She takes hold of my arm, walking right beside me.

I break away harshly.

'You're cheap,' I tell her. 'A cheap tart like Slimey said.' I mean it when I say it, but I don't mean to say it that way. Not in those exact words. Not like this. Even though I've got the right.

Melanie stands back, startled, the shock showing on her face. No! And now Lovett's heard it, as well. He comes over, an uncomfortable look on his face. *What am I still doing here?*

'Don't go just yet,' he says.

I can feel my face harden. I clench my fingers, nails cutting into the palms of my hands. I hate him and I want to hit him, but there's just no fighting spirit left in me. I'm not lowering myself to Slimey's level. Lovett's just not worth it either. My breath comes slowly now, my shoulders slump.

'Are you OK?' Lovett asks calmly.

'Aye, sir, you can massage my head gently with a sledgehammer if you like.' I look at him and say, 'I believed in you.'

'Joey . . .'

I shake my head. 'Save it, coach. I gave everything to the team. Our team. I trusted you.'

He sighs. 'I'm not proud of the way I've handled things. The last thing I wanted was to hurt or deceive you.'

'But you did, didn't you?'

'Don't blame yourself, Tristan,' Melanie tells him. 'It's all my fault.'

Lovett hesitates. 'It's not the way it seems, Joey.'

'So tell me then, 'cause I really want to know.'

Melanie speaks slowly now, honestly, holding nothing back. She admits that she used me to try and make Lovett jealous. She had asked him out last week, but he had said no, even though he had fancied her as well, because it was unprofessional to become involved with a pupil. He had told her she should go out with someone her own age. What better choice than the school hotshot . . . lucky for her, she says, that I asked her out when I did. My big gob, eh? That's why she jumped at the offer and was so keen to be seen with me. What she didn't know, and what I maybe should have told her, was that Slimey Climie was going to jump her boy-friend after the party. Any boyfriend – me or Lovett, as it turned out – it didn't matter to Slimey. If Slimey couldn't get the girl, then he could at least hospitalise her boyfriend. It didn't make any difference to him as long as he could save face and gain some sick satisfaction.

But Melanie didn't two-time anyone. Climie or me. And she didn't lead me on either. We barely touched hands, never mind had that first snog I've been dreaming about for weeks!

She knew I was crazy about her and that's why she deliberately kept her distance. I can see now that she only acted out of desperation 'cause she was scared the school authorities would think she was snogging a student teacher, even though they've only just got off with each other tonight.

It's unbelievable – but true. True love. It wasn't until Lovett was nearing the end of his teaching placement that they realised their feelings for each other. That's why things went further than a few late copy dates in the *School Voice* office. Of course it was Mel who Rab's brother saw in Lovett's car but he had only driven her home because it was dark outside by the time they had finished up for the night.

When I told Melanie at the party that Lovett was seeing another girl up in Glasgow, it made her all the more determined to get her man. That's why she was flirting with him all night, and why she went to help carry his presents to the car. And it was while they were saying goodbye to each other in the car park that Lovett finally gave into his feelings for Melanie. And that's where Slimey Climie came in, to spoil the party for everyone.

'We just didn't expect to fall in love,' Melanie's telling me. She smiles at Lovett who grins back at her.

But what about me? I want to be in love, as well. But I can't push it any more. I don't have the right now. I wasn't going out with Melanie, not really, even when I thought I was.

I turn, sighing, toward him. 'You must think

I'm a real plonker. I'm still acting like one now. I know I am. But I don't care. I trusted you. I trusted you both. I'm not hiding how I feel, felt, still feel . . .'

'Joey,' he says slowly. 'What we did to you was unforgivable. If anything, it's me who's been a plonker.'

I look at him, surprised to hear the words coming from his mouth. Why do you have to be so honest, sir? Can't you see I'm trying so hard to hate you. But I don't. Deep down, I don't. I know that. Forget the macho man image, my hurt male pride. Oh, I'm proud all right, but I'm proud enough to be as much as a man about this as I can. Even though I'm gutted inside. He's still a great bloke in my mind, that's the hardest part to accept. And Melanie's still gorgeous looking. She's a great girl, too. It's what's inside that counts. Even after what she did to me. What they both did to me.

There's this big sad empty feeling inside me that won't be going away for a while yet. But I'll get over it, won't I? The right girl for me is waiting just round the corner, isn't she? That's what Mel and Lovett have been trying to tell me. They're right. I know they are. Even though I still don't want to believe them.

In a way I'm grateful that he is going out with my dream girl – 'cause I realise that's all Melanie Anderson really is. A fantasy. Mel's not the girl for me – I know that now. The same as the film babe posters on my bedroom wall

258

could never ever be anything more to me than a healthy schoolboy's crush. It's all part of growing up, isn't it? I guess I'm still learning the rules of life and trying not to make too many mistakes as I go along.

But how embarrassing. What a cringer! The way I've been acting! And I don't know why I'm still feeling this way now, 'cause I know deep down that I'm not in love with Melanie. I never really was. I'm still pretty screwed-up, I can tell you!

Mad, crazy, crushy love just doesn't go away with a quick snap of the fingers, you know. In some ways it's like the pining pain I felt when my dad died – that I still feel now. I've grown up a lot in the last few weeks – and I've grown up even more tonight. I'm not going to say that Melanie Anderson hasn't left me feeling flat and disappointed and hurt and upset and angry still . . . 'cause it's a mixture of all these con-flicting emotions that has left this tight knot in the pit of my stomach now.

'I'm sorry,' Melanie says again, snuggling closer to Lovett. 'No hard feelings, Joey?'

Oh, I'm trying hard to hide my feelings, darlin'. But I smile at them, anyway, even though I'm torn apart inside.

'You'll go all the way to Hampden, Braveheart,' Lovett says. 'And I'll be proud to cheer you on . . . even if I have to pay to get in the bloody park!'

Melanie giggles. 'Well, Sally did say in her

259

interview that he was cute. And he'll soon be in all the teen mags, too, if she has anything to do with it.'

Cute? What kind of crummy word is that to use!

'Sally is a pretty good writer, huh?' I grin. 'She has a way with words, all right.'

'And she's also very pretty,' Melanie says, squeezing my hand softly. 'Haven't you seen the way she looks at you, Joey? Didn't you see the disappointment in her eyes when she left without you? I knew the moment I read her interview. The bits I had to cut from the article that appeared in the paper . . .' She giggles again. 'Sally was practically begging me to let her cover the story tonight. That's why I gave her the special Press Pass, when, rightfully, it should have gone to a more senior reporter.'

I think I know what Melanie's getting at here, but I'm not as hot about girls as I am on a football pitch, even if I like to pretend I am. I thought Sally and I just had a best mates bond between us, 'cause we're neighbours, like the brother-sister thing we've never known. I know Mel said love was waiting for me round the corner, but I didn't know she meant next door! She said I would find the right girl for me one day, but I didn't know she meant right now! All this time Sally's been trying to teach me the old lurve tricks for chicks, when what she was really doing was showing me the feelings she has for me. The sad-lad practising love god! I was getting all embarrassed about not understanding girls and opening up my feelings to her . . . while all the time Sally was trying to tell me how she really feels about me. About me! What *I'm* feeling now for *her*! How I felt in the party when I wanted to kiss her. How I've felt all along but didn't know you were supposed to. Is this what love is? The real kind of love? I've almost lost Sally when I didn't even know she was there – waiting for *me* all this time! But the Taylors are moving away. Her dad's got a new job in Dumfries. Sally's leaving!

'*Sally's in love with you,*' Melanie is saying, shaking me by the arm. 'You big dumb, stupid, cute . . . oh, go and get the girl, Braveheart! You're wasting time! Can't you see she's waiting on *you* to make the first move!'

And then I'm running from the car park and out into the street and calling over my shoulder, 'Good luck, you two! Hope it all works out for ya!'

And still I'm running.

I'm running, running.

38

Even before I reach the end of our street I can
see the lights are off in my house. I know that
Friday isn't a night my mum usually goes out
and I tell myself vaguely that she's probably
taking Laddie for a walk. But I'm not going
home just yet as I walk up the path and ring
another doorbell. The door opens, bringing the
drift of laughter and a familiar smell of aftershave I know only too well . . .

'Hello, Detective Sergeant—'

'I wish you would call me Bob . . . or at least
Mr Taylor.'

I've never seen Serious Sarge smiling before.
I didn't even know that *was* his name. The
initials on his detective kitbag are DS Taylor.
Oh, aye, Sarge . . .

'Not only do you make me feel like I'm still at
work,' he's saying, 'you make me feel old!'

'You're home, Joey!' My mum walks through
from the kitchen, waving to me, a glass of wine
in her hand. 'Wait till you hear the good news,
son.'

'We're staying put in Ardrossan,' Mr Taylor
says, still smiling.

Mrs Taylor joins the celebration. 'All my family and friends are here, Joey. And I know I'd miss your mum . . .'

'Isn't it wonderful, son? Isn't it great they're not going away after all?'

'*Where's Sally?*'

Silence.

The party's over for them as well. For a couple of seconds anyway . . .

My big gob!

'She said she was taking Laddie for a long walk. Down South Beach,' my mum says, grinning. 'Didn't she look a wee cracker in her new disco clothes, son?'

'Aye, *Maw.*'

And then I'm away again, bombing down the street.

39

When I get to South Beach, I find Sally sitting on a bench, alone; Laddie sniffing along the stretch of grass lit up by streetlights that goes all the way along the seaside promenade walk. Sally stands up when she sees me, but she doesn't say anything. She doesn't have to.

'I've been looking all over for ya,' I say. I hurry towards her, my heart pounding, pounding. 'There's something I have to tellya!'

I'm grinning away like a madman now and I don't even care who's banging their binoculars against the windows of all those lit up houses facing the shorefront. Why didn't I see it before? Why was I so blind? Those little tell-tale looks of Sally's with their hidden tender meanings, the awkward moments between us that left me feeling something I never knew could make you feel so good inside if you only give it a chance. If only I knew! Real love. Not the mistaken crush I've had on Melanie Anderson. The love that was staring me straight in the face all this time.

I take Sally in my arms – just like they do in the movies – and look into her laughing eyes that are sparkling with the still-damp sheen of tears.

'I think I fancy ya, Sal.'

'*Fancy*?'

'Aye, Sal . . . fancy *fancy*, if you know what I mean?'

She pushes me away. 'No, I don't know what you mean, Joey Burns?'

'I love you, OK! I love you!' I hold my arms out, hiding nothing now. 'I love you.'

Sally pulls me towards her. 'Oh, I know that. I've always known that.'

'Ya have? Why didn'tcha tell me?' I stare at her, suddenly understanding something else as well. 'You *knew* you weren't leaving? At the party. That's *why* yer dad got the journo cards printed.'

'Oooh, you're so *slow* sometimes.' She puts her arms round my neck, pulling me closer. 'This is the bit when *you're* supposed to kiss *me*, moron!'

And I do. For a long time. Until we both break away, gasping for breath. I hold her smiling face in my hands, finally seeing those soft, pretty features for the very first time. I look into Sally's big brown mischievous eyes – even if they do mean trouble. 'Oh, I love you, I love you,' I say again and again until I don't even know I've stopped telling her. I'm in love. Real love. True love. Mad love. I'm in love!

Sally looks at me and says, smiling, 'Ya gonna put yer tongue in or not?'

'No way,' I say. 'Ya might be more mature than me . . . but yer still too young!'

'I've loved you all my life, Joey Burns. So I suppose I can wait a little longer . . .' She kicks me sharply in the shin. 'Till ya grow up.'

'Ouch! That *hurt.*'

'We might not be moving away after all, hotshot. But I'll soon be going to college in Glasgow to study journalism. And when I graduate and become a reporter for the teen mags, I'll be covering more than just the Scotland games at the World Cup.' She draws my big dumb, stupid, cute head down to hers. 'So ya'd better get yer other act together as well, Braveheart.'

We kiss again. A long, slow, dreamy kind of kiss that seems to last forever. This one *really* takes my breath away. Oh, I might be the hottest football talent in Ayrshire, all right, but I know what the final score is now: I can never win with Sally Taylor!

And then Laddie jumps up . . . *his* tongue all over us, his tail wagging with doggy approval.

'The home team,' I say.

'The home team,' Sally says.

And Laddie barks, too.